# Are You Nuts?

▶ ◀

# By Mark Richard Zubro

### THE "TOM AND SCOTT" MYSTERIES

*A Simple Suburban Murder*
*Why Isn't Becky Twitchell Dead?*
*The Only Good Priest*
*The Principal Cause of Death*
*An Echo of Death*
*Rust on the Razor*
*Are You Nuts?*

### THE "PAUL TURNER" MYSTERIES

*Sorry Now?*
*Political Poison*
*Another Dead Teenager*
*The Truth Can Get You Killed*

# Are
# You
# Nuts?

Mark Richard Zubro

St. Martin's Press
New York

Library of Congress Cataloging-in-Publication Data

Zubro, Mark Richard.
    Are you nuts? / by Mark Richard Zubro.
       p.    cm.
    ISBN 0-312-18528-6
    I. Title.
PS3576.U225A89   1998
813'.54—dc21                    98-11456
                                        CIP

First Edition: July 1998

10  9  8  7  6  5  4  3  2  1

*To Barb, Hugh, and Rick*

# Are
# You
# Nuts?

# , 1 ,

Beatrix Xury rushed into my classroom.

Beatrix lived to panic and her life bounced from one red alert to another. Beatrix was tall, thin, and mean. She'd been teaching at Grover Cleveland High School for nearly thirty-five years. She had taught the high-honors math class for ages, and during this time, she had directed the math team to innumerable state championships. Parents adored her. Their children shone brilliantly. Administrators usually started out loving her dearly, but after a few encounters, began hating her passionately. She nagged about anything. She complained about everything from the unbelievably trivial to the incredibly useless. Her incessant yammering could drive a roomful of saints nuts.

Firing her would be impossible. All those lovely math-team headlines? The inertia inherent in any school system bureaucracy? Add those to the fact that she didn't physically abuse any children, and she'd be entrenched in her position until the sun and moon switched orbits. Students had wildly mixed reactions to her. If she liked you, class and the math team were pure heaven. If she disliked you, you got a taste of total hell.

As a fellow faculty member, I'd avoided her for years.

As the union building representative in the recent past, I'd tried my best to sidestep the worst of her nuttiness. Being building rep also meant handling grievances for my building. At these, Beatrix excelled. Always go with your strength.

At the end of last year, I had wanted to quit my dual role. Kurt Campbell, our union president and a good friend, had begged me not to. Normally, I'm sensible enough to refuse Kurt's more extreme requests—dealing with loony people is not a favorite pastime of mine. However, at the age of thirty-nine, he'd needed quadruple heart bypass surgery. On a visit to him in the hospital just before school was let out last spring, he'd told me he was going to resign as union president. He said he wanted to leave the organization in good hands and suggested I run for union president. I'm not that nuts. I'd had the sense to say no even with his promise of full support in the special election to be held just after school started in August. After I turned down his suggestion on the presidency, he'd convinced me that certain key positions had to be held by competent people he trusted. How can you refuse a friend who's flat on his back after having major surgery?

At the moment, he was relaxing with his wife and kids in some spa in Arizona owned by his parents. I couldn't wait for him to get back. Which left me several days before school began that August sitting in an unair-conditioned classroom listening to Beatrix Xury. She had pale skin and blue-rinsed, long hair pulled back and tied in a bun. Her lips compressed firmly when she was miffed or concerned. When startled or angry, her face took on the look of someone who had just had a large pickle jammed up her ass.

Beatrix was a special case. At the drop of the most trivial mote of a problem, she would call me. At home. Constantly. Usually after 10 P.M. Why Beatrix couldn't have a crisis at seven or eight in the evening was beyond me. She'd call about the fact that members of her department wouldn't share their computers. That they didn't invite her to parties. That other teachers had classes with brighter kids or easier electives to teach. That her pet projects never received any budget money. That every other teacher had more office space than she. That the district was infringing on her academic freedom. (This last a neat trick in a math class.) Or if all these didn't work, she used the general complaint of "it's not fair."

This Monday in August, her opening salvo after she burst into my room was, "You've got to go to the PTA meeting tonight."

I sighed.

She prattled on, "They're going to pay a nontenured teacher to organize the senior-honors math-team field trip to the national math convention this year. That's not fair. I've done it all these years for nothing. I said I wouldn't do it again unless I was paid. So, they told me they'd find somebody else, but now they're paying somebody." To a teacher such as Beatrix, with years of seniority in the district along with an attitude problem, allowing a newer teacher even the slightest privilege was one of the greatest sins.

On this issue, I was particularly unsympathetic. First, she'd used the dreaded chant of the nineties—it's not fair. Second, she'd used the other F-word. I hate field trips. I can't imagine going anywhere with any group of fifty people on an uncomfortable bus. Field trips are little more than madness in action. Fill a bus with teenagers and drag them to something an adult has decided is educational, and they will be bored to tears and ready for more kinds of mischief than I would ever choose to imagine. You want to go on a field trip, don't get near me.

"How is this a violation of the union contract?" I asked. (What I wanted to say was, "Listen, you silly twit. That is incredibly stupid, selfish, moronic, and against your own self-interest." I've discovered that truth can be a highly overrated commodity.)

"They can't be paying someone without going through the union. That's not right."

I wished it were possible to tell her about the teacher who had been in half an hour earlier, but I'd been sworn to secrecy. A parent had cornered this teacher and said that she was going to call the police and file child-molestation charges against the teacher. No matter that the teacher had never had the child in class, didn't know who the child was, had never met the child, and had never molested any child. I'd set this teacher up with a meeting with the union lawyer. Wishing her good luck as she had left had hardly seemed enough. A tragedy in the making, and now here was Beatrix with this nonsensical trash.

Tact with my colleagues. That's what Scott always reminds me about. But I've said it a million times. I can have incredible amounts of patience with the teenagers I teach, but I expect adults to act like adults, a proposition at least as chancy as that of always speaking the truth.

"How is offering someone money above what the contract pays not right?" I asked.

"Of course it isn't right. How could it be? They can't do that. They've never done it before."

"How much money is involved?"

"It isn't the amount, it's the principle of the thing."

Which meant it wasn't going to be a lot. Isn't that the way it always is? People get mad and claim it's a "principle" when most of the time what they mean is that it's a petty nothing that they've chosen to take as an insult. And usually when something big is a real insult, they chicken out about doing something about it.

I had a million things to do this day. I hadn't gotten a chance to get into my classroom earlier, and I had tons of work to do. Since I'd returned home, I'd had meetings each day. I was not in the mood for this crap.

I asked again, "How much?"

"One hundred dollars."

Beatrix's salary was at least $65,000 a year. For little more than chump change, she would parade herself and her silly complaint before anybody she could corral. The result of her carrying on would not be new freedom and dignity for the oppressed masses of teachers. Unfortunately, many of her colleagues would not conclude she was a total moron. Rather, she would be hailed for fighting for her rights. I didn't care if she exercised her right to be stupid. I just wished she wouldn't do it near me.

What Beatrix didn't know was that I already knew about her problem. The school principal had called as a courtesy last week to inform me of the change and Beatrix's probable upset. I'd met with several union officials about this and a number of other issues last Friday. Years ago, when I first accepted this job, they'd told me what to watch out for, excuses people would give, pitfalls to avoid, and possible options to pursue. Unfortunately, blasting Beatrix into space for a long trip to Jupiter was not possible.

As for Beatrix's immediate problem, I'd discovered that no one had ever asked her to set up the field trip. Each year she'd complained about not being paid, and each year, union officials, her department chair, her colleagues, and probably her pet fish had told her—if she had so much to complain about, then simply cancel the damn trip, but no.

"You've got to file a grievance," she declared.

"Against whom?"

"The PTA."

I stifled my first comment. "Are you nuts?" certainly was the appropriate question. What I said, patiently, was, "The PTA is not part of our contract."

"They can't just start paying people. It's not fair."

In that humidity-infested room, I said, "Well, Beatrix, you'll have to fill out the paperwork." I'd discovered that giving in sometimes drives them nuts. Better them going crazy than me.

Now she said, "Why can't the union file the grievance? Why do I have to?"

This was a fairly common tactic among those faculty who loved to cause trouble but didn't want to get off their butts. If they really believed in the cause they were championing, they'd do whatever it took to right the wrong done to them. Too often they simply loved the upset and uproar that gave somebody else headaches. They had a problem, but you had to do all the work.

I said, "You know how it works, Beatrix. The union helps the member on the grievance. We go with them to meetings. We give advice and assist in writing grievances. We represent them, but the member has to take the responsibility."

"I don't see why you can't do it."

"I'm not sure I'm capable of making you see why, Beatrix. I don't know what you want from me."

"Do something! Talk to them. Go to the meeting."

"This is not something for the union to be involved in.

It does not concern the union. When someone offers us more money, it is not a bad thing to say yes. We have no control over what the PTA does. There is no case here. The union doesn't have a leg to stand on."

"You sound just like an administrator. The union's never done anything for me. They just take my dues every year. They don't really care what happens to me. I'm going to quit the union."

I blew it big time by responding, "Yes, please do."

Sometimes when they find out the union can't fix their problem, they threaten to drop their membership. They definitely believe in the what-have-you-done-for-me-lately theory of political interaction.

Half my time was spent telling teachers they didn't have a case. They'd insist that I call Kurt, the union-local office, God Almighty, or someone with an equal amount of power as God Almighty in order to try to find any little opening that might allow them to tell their boss to shove it.

I regretted my injudicious comment to Beatrix almost as soon as I made it.

First, she got teary eyed. Then she sputtered a few seconds. Then she stomped to the exit, turned, and declared, "I'm getting my own lawyer." She punctuated her departure with a slamming of the door.

Sometimes when you didn't tell teachers what they wanted to hear, they threatened to get their own lawyer. Ninety-nine percent of the time, you never heard from them or their lawyer.

I looked around my classroom. From walls and ceilings Beatrix had loosened specks of dust that still drifted down in the sticky air.

The wing of the school that contained my old classroom had burned down. They had shifted the English department to the oldest remaining wing of Grover Cleveland. This was not a good thing. I now had a chalkboard that was old-fashioned black, chipped, and paint-stained. The filth-encrusted windows gave an unimpeded view of the pothole-infested faculty parking lot. They'd unbent far enough to polish the tile floor of my classroom. This was a dubious benefit. No matter how often they scrubbed or how much cleaner they used on the ugly-grayish, dingy-yellow floor, the accumulated dirt never seemed to go away.

I needed to get to work on my classroom. The walls were still bare. None of the books, tests, reading centers, tapes, and other materials for the year had been unpacked. The computer, movable cart, modem, CD-ROM, and television set were still in their boxes. As a birthday gift last year, Scott had upgraded my electronic equipment in our penthouse. These were the perfectly usable leftovers. Despite my legitimate method of obtaining all this, I could already hear Beatrix and her ilk saying "it wasn't fair" that I got a computer and they didn't. Ask me if I cared.

The summer had been unbelievably hectic. My lover, Scott Carpenter, and I had run from interview to interview about his being an openly gay baseball player. The talk shows listed us as the "happy gay couple." Right now a cozy little hideaway with Scott and me and food and water for six months would have been nice. Scott was still on the road and not due back for several more days. I'd come home to begin the school year. Part of the problem in dealing with Beatrix had been the dissonance I felt between the national attention I'd received for something I thought of as supremely important and the unbelievable unimportance of her complaints.

I was sure I would hear more about my crack to Beatrix, but I wasn't going to get worried about it yet. I had too much to do to waste time brooding on it.

I hunted for my old lesson-plan book where, in the front, I keep the assembled notes from past years about things to do for the opening of school. Most I could remember with my eyes closed, but if I didn't check the list, I always forgot something. I knew that at least I wanted to get the kids' names typed into my computer grade-book program today.

I searched for fifteen minutes, but I couldn't find the lesson-plan book. I looked through all the cabinets, then through every box of materials I'd accumulated over the years. It wasn't serious that it was gone, but it was odd. I always put it in the same "safe" place. Now I was worried that I'd found a new "safe" place and forgotten it. I knew I had it somewhere, it was just a matter of digging until it turned up. But it didn't. After half an hour, I gave up and opened the first box of computer equipment to look for the instruction manual.

Fifteen minutes later, Meg Swarthmore strolled into the room. "Now what have you done?"

Meg works part-time in the library at Grover Cleveland. She used to be head librarian but is now semiretired. At the beginning and end of the year, she works full-time helping to set up or take down all the materials. She is the ultimate clearinghouse for all school gossip. She'd tried giving up the telling-secrets business several years ago. Referring to her return as gossip central, she had said, "Living for cheap, tawdry gossip might not be as good as dying for chocolate, but it'll do until you get your next candy bar." We had been good friends for years. She was not much over five feet tall and was plump in a grandmotherly way.

She's in her sixties and could have retired years ago, but she loves books and kids. As for the gossip, she had one basic rule: never reveal a source.

I dusted my hands to clean off the classroom grime that always seemed to accumulate on everything over the summer. With a minimum of effort, they could create a Dust Hall of Fame or a Dust Museum out of the school.

"Done what?" I asked.

"Beatrix is in tears."

"I'm a beast."

"I saw her talking with Jon Pike." Jon was the new head of the English department. I'd known him for years as an officious bore/colleague. In the last year, he'd become officious bore/head of the department. He ran boring departmental meetings during which he'd parrot boring Shakespeare quotes at oddly inappropriate times.

"Jon will certainly be a big help. Before and after he became head of the department, he was always willing to throw gasoline on a fire."

"What did you say to Beatrix?"

"I tried telling her no." I told Meg about the field-trip money. "Beatrix wouldn't listen. She told me 'it wasn't fair.' To my credit, I did not call flaming destruction down from heaven on her."

"Can you do that?"

"What?"

"The flaming whatsis?"

"Only on a really good day. When she threatened to quit the union, I said, 'Please do.' "

"You didn't?"

"I did."

Meg burst out into hysterical laughter. She had to sit in the chair behind my desk and hold her sides before she got herself back under control. She wiped her eyes and said, "I would pay to have a video of that moment. You could sell it and make a fortune."

"I thought I was a model of calm objectivity."

"We may need to work with you on that," Meg said.

"What could I have done better? I didn't yell or scream. I didn't call her names. I only gave her a dose of truth, which she did not want. I said what every other union rep has wanted to say to her for years. If anybody else wants this job, they are welcome to it."

"I don't suspect there will be a stampede to be grievance chair." She shook her head. "Beatrix is an injustice collector, which is kind of sad. You know she wasn't always goofy. A year or two before you started teaching in the district, her husband died of a rare type of cancer and left her with two daughters who weren't even in grade school yet. She wasn't as driven before that. She was your average, mostly eager teacher. The death changed her."

"Now, I do feel like a heel."

"She is a nag and an asshole. Yeah, you'll probably get negative repercussions for what you said. You want to worry needlessly about it? I've always thought paralytic catatonia was an interesting response to stimuli."

"That's probably not helpful here. I've got plenty of other stuff to be concerned about."

Meg got up from the chair and plunked herself on a corner of my worn and battered desk. "Speaking of things to worry about, if we can manage to save you from Beatrix's wrath, I do have hot gossip."

"The best kind."

"Which I'm afraid has some unpleasant elements in it. Did you know that this evening there's an election for PTA officers?"

"Somehow it slipped my mind."

"Well, there is. These things are important."

"To whom?"

"You want gossip or you want to make caustic comments?"

"Gossip."

"You remember the huge fight during the last school board election?"

"Yeah."

Some of that fight had been a nasty set-to with stealth candidates from the religious right trying to sweep out four incumbents. With the strong support of the union, three out of four of the old guard had won. But an even deeper, more hidden agenda had not been revealed until later. Old wounds that many thought might have been healed were reopened. Ancient angers and enmities in the community had been renewed, and the new scars were not expected to heal for years, if ever. I knew Meg had been deeply involved in the election.

"Lydia Marquez, the religious right candidate now on the school board, has organized her buddies for tonight's PTA meeting. The election of officers occurs at the first get-together in August. She was going to pack the meeting to vote in her people."

"Democracy in action."

"Well, word got out. Phone lines are burning up in River's Edge even as I speak, summoning the faithful to tonight's meeting."

"I'm still not sure I care."

"Will it make a difference if I tell you the leading candidate for president is making you one of the big issues in her campaign?"

I was also concerned about the reactions to my notoriety among the students, faculty, and parents in the community. Would my celebrity status and extravagantly open gay presence cause ripples? I'd been on national television over half the summer with my lover. I'd have been foolish not to expect a backlash.

"Who is Lydia's candidate?"

"Belutha Muffin."

"Never heard of her."

"Well, she's heard of you, and she does not like you one itty-bit."

"Is there such a thing as two itty-bits?"

Meg ignored my comment. "You should see Belutha in action."

"Is she a deadly raving loony?"

"No, she comes across as Ms. Sunshine and Lollipop. She speaks mostly in mindless slogans. She always brings a laptop computer and a projection screen to show pithy slogans at the meetings she goes to. Once she brought a videotape filled with sunshine and flowers."

"That doesn't sound criminal."

"Insulting to anyone with a modicum of sense. I'd love to see that simpering smile wiped off her face," Meg said.

"Sounds like you've got problems with her."

"For years. I think I better go to the meeting."

"Should I?" I asked.

"If you're going to be a subject of debate, it might be better not to. If you show up, you could become a flash point."

"I could also defend myself."

"Either way, it may not be pretty. You wouldn't be able to sit quietly on the side. If they don't know you from school, they'll recognize who you are from the television shows."

"I could wear a disguise."

"You could try the flaming-destruction-from-heaven trick."

"Cool."

# 2

Carolyn Blackburn walked into the room. She'd been superintendent of the River's Edge School District for several years now, and before that she'd been principal of Grover Cleveland High School. She'd been a decent boss and I'd trusted her more than any other school administrator, which really doesn't say much. Carolyn was a heavyset woman with silver hair and a broad, pleasant face that at the moment was packed with worried frown lines.

Meg said to her, "You look frazzled."

"Meetings with lawyers and more lawyers. We've got three separate lawsuits against the district and another in the offing. Time was, you could run a school district and expect not to be front-page news."

"It's not worth all those big bucks they pay you?" I asked.

"They don't mint enough money on the planet to make it worthwhile," she replied. Her frown deepened. "I saw you on a few television shows this summer."

"I missed them myself. My parents even had cable television and a satellite dish installed so they could tape some of the more obscure ones. I'm afraid they're going to make copies for everyone I know."

She grinned briefly. "I admire your courage. I hope you and your lover are okay."

"Doing about average, I guess."

She nodded, then resumed frowning. "You've heard about the PTA meeting tonight?"

"Just now."

"You need me to leave?" Meg asked.

"That isn't necessary. Tom, your situation is more volatile than I'd imagined. We did get a large number of calls over the summer as you were on more and more shows. After the *Oprah* appearance, the phones didn't stop for a week. These were mostly complaints. Oddly and fortunately, most of them were not from parents in the district, but this Belutha person is dead set on getting you fired."

"The PTA has the strength to hire and fire teachers?"

"Of course not. But it's pressure on the school board that they're after. Politics—local or national—is about pressure."

"I appreciate the help you've been over the years, Carolyn, but I'm not fighting about being in the closet here. If the school board wants to take action, I'll call my lawyer, the ACLU, and the Lambda Legal Defense Fund."

"This time it may come to that. I can't stop the PTA or the board. I still think you are an excellent teacher and an asset to this district. I will do what I can to protect you. Maybe nothing will happen. This board may have been re-elected with a lot of union help, but they are an independent lot. It's a good thing I'm only a year or two from retirement or I'd resign. I may anyway."

"Why quit?" Meg asked.

"The board is out of control. School boards are supposed to set policy and make sure the money is spent responsibly and according to the law. Presumably they leave the day-to-day running of the district to the administrators. Is that how you've seen things happen around here lately? They've been trying to micromanage the school district, and they haven't the slightest idea what they're doing. An administrator has to feel free to make decisions, not have a board constantly looking over her shoulder playing a game of 'gotcha.' "

I'd never known a superintendent to be so frankly honest.

"Please don't quit," Meg said. "You're too good an administrator and too sane."

Carolyn smiled. "Which is why I don't know why I'm still in education." She left.

"If she's worried, so am I," Meg said.

"Let's keep this in perspective," I said. "While my job is important to me, and I will certainly fight to keep it, losing my job would not be a total tragedy. I've saved money over the years, and Scott is a bit beyond very wealthy. If I get fired, we're not going to be eating gruel anytime soon."

"Did you talk to Scott last night?"

"For quite a while. I miss him."

"Before the baseball strike, he was gone on road trips for longer than this."

"But this is harder for him. Pitching is something he's done since he was a little kid. Being a celebrity spokesperson, 'out' athlete, and talk show denizen takes an emotional toll. He's hurting. Most of the time on the tour, we'd spend evenings into early mornings talking or holding each other. It wasn't passion or sex, but just a desire to comfort and soothe. He's worried about ever pitching again, being on the mound the first time and every time after, with hostile fans prepared to physically harm him."

"That's got to be rough for both of you, but Scott isn't the first one playing has been tough for. I remember Jackie Robinson. How'd he get through it?"

"People of goodwill, someone who loved him. Scott has that."

"Will it be enough?"

"I wish I knew. What makes dealing with this worse is the radical gay groups who insist that he has to go out and pitch no matter what the cost. He could be injured or killed but they don't care. They want him as poster boy, martyr. I think some of them want to bring him down as well."

"I don't understand."

"The jealous queens who've scrambled for their piece of the five o'clock news see Scott as coming out of nowhere and horning in on their turf."

"But Scott can do so much good."

"But petty jealousy is often the rule of the day. You know the Chicago gay newspapers have had almost no coverage of any of this. Only after the *Chicago Tribune,* the *Chicago Sun-Times,* and *The New York Times* had special articles on him did they even mention his coming out."

"A prophet is without honor in his own country."

"Or maybe they're just fucking morons."

"There is that."

I glanced into one of the boxes of computer materials. "I'm never going to get any of this done. I've got an orientation meeting at noon with all the union building reps. Then one of the candidates for union president wants to meet with me. He wants my endorsement. Although with me being a controversial figure, I'm not sure my word is going to mean much."

"You've got to remember most of the staff around here have known you're gay for years and are pretty accepting.

You may be more famous now, but you're still the person they know. You still command great respect. And there's a cachet to your being famous, which adds its own luster."

"I've been feeling really lusterful lately."

"Some people have all the luck. Who you back in the election could be important. People care passionately about who is in charge of the union, and bitter feelings can last for years. Who are you backing in the election?"

"Neither one so far."

"Why not?"

"I haven't heard anything impressive about either one. I heard each one claim he's committed to equal rights for all teachers, so it's a wash on gay rights. What does your gossip grapevine say about the two of them?"

"You know Jerome Blenkinsop in the math department here?"

"I've been on one or two union committees with Jerome, but I don't know him well. I've never met the elementary candidate, Seth O'Brien."

"They both grew up in the Chicago area. Seth's been in the district eight or nine years. He's taking graduate courses in computer science at Governors State, I think. He graduated from UCLA. Jerome's been here at least ten years longer than you have. He got his undergrad degree at USC. I guess neither one was enamored enough of California to stay there."

"Somebody has to like these winters."

"Yeah. Let's see. Both are married. Seth has a preschool-age child. Jerome's are older, maybe one or two in college. Both men are reputed to be friendly enough to work with. No affairs. Jerome's taken a variety of courses in numerous master's degree programs over the years. Never stuck with any one long enough to graduate. He's been involved in a lot of causes in the community for quite a while. I'll try to find out more."

"Kurt hasn't endorsed either one. I wish he was staying in charge."

"Rumor has it that Seth wants to fight to dump all the tenure laws."

"Is he nuts?"

"That's the rumor."

"That he's nuts or that he wants to dump the tenure laws?"

"Probably both. I was going to suggest dinner tonight, but I think I better go to this meeting. You'll need a first-hand account, and I may need to lend my leather-lunged warble to the debate. I still live in this district. I've got a vote and a voice."

"You're a member of the PTA?"

"Actually, you are too. Everybody on the staff is. It's part of the Social Club dues you pay twenty-five bucks to every year."

"It is?"

"You betcha. It sounds like serious issues and person-alities are going to be on the line tonight. I've got friends that I can call."

"Is it that serious? A PTA can't have that much power."

"You heard Carolyn. I think she's right."

"I'm more worried about Scott than about what either the PTA or the school board will do. I've been making these brave statements all these years about not living in fear. I guess this will be the big fight."

"Possibly. People love to intrude where their noses don't belong. The meeting isn't just about you though. There are other issues besides you."

"I wonder if Edwina is going to the meeting."

Edwina Jenkins was the school principal. After teaching for a number of years, she'd gotten her administrative certificate and worked her way up through the ranks.

Meg used her pet name for Edwina. "Shit-for-brains probably has to show up. She's as useless as any administrator we've ever had."

"Try not to hold back, Meg. Let me know how you really feel."

"I guess she tells as many lies as any administrator. If she shows up, she won't be any help. I'm definitely going. I love a good fight once in a while. I'm in the mood to be nasty to a few people." She stood up. "I've got to finish cataloging the new books that arrived over the summer. As well as plot, plan, and connive about tonight's meeting."

I told her I would join her later to discuss strategy and possibly help make phone calls.


Half an hour later, I'd assembled the computer equipment. This was progress. When it was new, it had taken me half a day and three calls to the "help line" before I mastered the on switch. Next, I searched for my computer disks. I have a small collection that I use both at home and on the departmental computers that we share. I found the disks strewn in the back of my cabinet. I knew I hadn't left them there. I thought about hunting for the custodians to find out who had been in my room and why my stuff had gotten messed with. Was it important enough?

My next visitor was Seth O'Brien. I was not expecting him. I had a meeting with Jerome set for two that afternoon.

"Can we talk?" he asked.

I let the computer hum to itself and gave him my attention. Seth was in his late twenties. He was tall and heavyset, maybe a defensive lineman for a smaller college. He wore a loose T-shirt without any logo, baggy shorts, and sandals with white socks. Prior to Meg's information, I'd known he taught third graders in one of the elementary schools in the district. I'd heard he was a competent teacher.

"What can I do for you?" I asked.

"I'm hoping to get your endorsement in the election," he said.

"I can't imagine my word is very important. With all the controversy surrounding Scott, my name isn't going to be something to hang on a banner."

"People respect you, Tom. Members of the faculty listen to what you have to say. Your reputation is solid."

"Thank you for the kind words. I'm not sure who I favor for president."

"I think the elementary teachers in this district have been ignored for too long. We need to do more for them."

"What hasn't Kurt done?"

"You high school teachers are always trying to run things. All the union officers are from the high school. All that extra money is spent for high school sports. We never get anything."

"Did you ever discuss this with Kurt?"

"No."

"Why haven't you volunteered to be on the negotiations team? Why haven't you come to any of the meetings?"

"We're discussing it now. The problem with the transfer situation in this district is horrendous. In all the years

Kurt has been president, not one elementary teacher has been given a job in the high school."

This was a sore spot in many unit districts. Many elementary teachers saw upper-grade and high school jobs as more prestigious. As grievance chair and building rep, I didn't deal with any interschool hassles. "Have any of the elementary teachers applied for the jobs?"

"Of course. It's not fair the way the elementary teachers have been treated in this district."

He'd used the magic words—*it's not fair.* I'd heard that refrain so often I was more than sick of it. Besides the obvious response of "life is not fair," there were other problems with it. Too often when people say "it's not fair," what they really mean is "I'm not getting my way." Further, by overusing "it's not fair," that which is truly "not fair" becomes trivial. I didn't have the energy to get in a big fight with him about it, but I did ask, "What other things are the elementary teachers upset about, and why, if they are so important, weren't they brought up to Kurt before this?"

He said, "Planning time. High school teachers have more planning time than we do. We teach far more subjects than they do. They only have to plan for one or two subjects. We've got over a dozen. That's not fair."

"I hear you're in favor of ending all the tenure laws."

"Yes."

"Are you nuts?"

"There are too many unqualified teachers in the schools."

"Do you understand what tenure means?" I didn't give him a chance to answer. "For public-school teachers in this state, it simply means they have to give you due process before they can fire you. It means an administrator has to tell a teacher what they are doing wrong and give them a chance to fix it within ninety days. How is that a burden?"

"The teachers' unions are out of control."

"And you want to be the head of one? Are you nuts?"

"I think we should have the IEA come in here instead of the IFT."

This referred to an old feud between the Illinois Education Association and the Illinois Federation of Teachers. For years there had been bad blood, "raids," and nasty feuds between the two groups. Fortunately, for the past few years the two groups had been having merger talks and had signed a "no raid" agreement. That meant neither group would try to get the other out as the exclusive bargaining agent in any school district. I remembered vaguely we'd had some problems like this many years before I started teaching at Grover Cleveland. The way I saw the merger talks was that they gave chronic complainers one less threat to make when they were pissed off.

Battles between teachers could leave scars and wounds that might never heal. I explained to Seth about the "no raid" agreement.

His response was, "It doesn't hurt to talk to them."

I wasn't in the mood to argue, and I didn't see this discussion as going anywhere, but I was curious. "Are you going to the PTA meeting tonight?"

I caught him off guard. "I don't think the union needs to be involved in that kind of controversy."

"Which kind?"

"You know, with elections. I don't think we should have endorsed anyone in the past school board races. Look how that Belutha Muffin has turned against us."

"I don't remember her ever being for us. We could have

had three more just like her if we hadn't endorsed anybody."

"I don't know that. Those people who are supposedly on our side might have won anyway."

"Or maybe not. I wasn't willing to take a chance. How can someone be union president without going out on a limb sometimes?"

"Obviously you do take chances. I know that at least one of the PTA candidates has been talking about you and your friend being on all those television shows. You probably shouldn't have been."

"Why not?"

"It stirs people up. Makes it harder to defend you."

"I'm not hiding in anybody's closet."

"Well, that's your decision."

I wanted to end this interview and get back to work. I said, "I have an appointment with your opponent this afternoon. For now, I'm holding off endorsing anyone in the election."

"No matter who wins, I'd like to see you remain as grievance chair."

I love politics. Whether it's on a national scale or a little local union election, it's favors, promises, and compromises. I laughed outright. "Seth, I'd be happy to let you have the job starting right now."

He edged farther toward the door. "Well, no. I just . . . Well . . . We can talk about it after the election." He scuttled out.

His performance just then did not endear him to me. I began to think about the possibility of endorsing his opponent. The next person who said "it's not fair" near me better be wearing a suit of armor.

I turned to begin dragging more computer equipment out of the boxes.

At noon I met with the building reps and several officials from the union-local office. The reps got the standard patter about do's and don'ts. I'd heard it before, so I tuned a lot of it out. No one made mention of Scott, celebrity status, television shows, Beatrix Xury, or the PTA. Good.

# 3

After lunch I returned to my classroom preparations. I was wearing an old pair of cutoff jeans, calf-length white socks, athletic shoes, and a T-shirt with the Grover Cleveland logo—a tyrannosaurus rex. Wherever cloth touched body, I was sweating. I could feel moisture bead on my forehead and form pools under my armpits. I'd have to remember to bring a fan from home tomorrow to try to beat back the oppressive heat. The central office area of Grover Cleveland High School was air-conditioned but not the rest of the school. They claimed it was too expensive to fix the old system or buy a new one, but it sure looks odd when you take care of the administration and no one else.

For about twenty minutes, I worked in blessed silence, then a noise at the door drew my attention. A lanky, blond male stood in the doorway. He wore tennis shoes with white, ankle-length socks, gauzy, white running shorts, and a black T-shirt cut at the midriff to reveal a flat stomach. The remaining portion of the T-shirt had the name of a heavy-metal rock group in lurid red letters.

"Students aren't allowed in the building yet," I said.

He came far enough into the room so that the windows backlit his torso. The light showed through the flimsy material of his shorts and outlined his legs up to his crotch. "I'm not a student. My name is Trevor Thompson. I'm a second-year teacher here in the math department. Are you Tom Mason?"

I said I was. With so many teachers in the school, it wasn't odd I didn't recognize him—especially a first- or second-year teacher. You seldom met other faculty members unless you had a planning period or ate lunch with them. Normally you knew your fellow department members and that was it.

Trevor had short, brush-cut hair and didn't look as if he needed to shave but once or twice a week. He glanced back at the door, then edged toward me. His voice was soft and low. "I wanted to talk to you. I'm worried about my job. I don't have tenure and I'm gay. I'm trying to find out what's going to happen."

I left the computer stuff and plopped myself on the ledge next to the open window. He sat in a student desk. He rested his left ankle on his right knee. The angle at which he sat afforded me a view all the way up his shorts to his skimpy jockstrap. He noticed my glance, slumped lower in the chair, and opened his legs wider, providing a more extensive panorama of his lower torso. I felt as if I was in the presence of a youthful Mrs. Robinson wanna-be. For a further display of his masculine charms, he entwined his fingers and rested them behind his head. This emphasized his flat stomach and narrow hips.

I asked, "What can I do for you?"

"I was working in my room today. I stopped in the lounge and I heard some of the faculty talking about you. I saw you on television this summer. You're really brave."

"I never expected to be on any talk show or be anybody's spokesperson. I'm not sure I ever want to be again.

I'm afraid my renown is due more to circumstance than it is bravery or wanting to fight the world."

He leaned forward and rested his elbows on his knees. "But you live with Scott Carpenter. That is so cool. Every gay guy I know is jealous. Everybody wants to know what he's like."

"Is that why you're here?"

"No, not really, but knowing the lover of Scott Carpenter is way cool."

I gazed at him silently. He shifted in his chair and gave me the spread-leg crotch-shot again. I kept my eyes on his as the silence lengthened beyond a comfortable few moments. I waited for him to speak. Finally, he cleared his throat, then said, "I'm most concerned about my job. I'm worried that if they find out I'm gay, they won't give me tenure. I heard something was going to happen at tonight's PTA meeting."

"The PTA doesn't grant tenure."

"They can cause trouble."

"People make all kinds of promises and threats."

"You can be that calm and detached?"

"Sometimes."

"Aren't you worried?"

"A little."

"Of course, with a rich lover, you don't have to worry at all."

"Which is none of your business."

"I'm sorry. I'm just scared. I bought a house and a new car. Without a job, I can't make those payments. I don't have a lover to fall back on. And yeah, I was curious to meet you. You're the most famous gay person in the country right now, you and your lover."

"I'd prefer less notoriety and simply teaching."

"But isn't it fun being on all the talk shows?"

"Look, I'm only a schoolteacher living with a man I love. If I'm lucky, the world will be a little better for that."

"You're never going to be just a guy."

The silence began to build again. Finally, Trevor said, "They made me be an assistant coach on the football team."

"So?"

"Can they do that? I teach math. I ran track in high school and college. I was maybe better than average, but that doesn't qualify me to coach football. I really don't want to do that."

"They didn't assign you any extracurricular duties your first year?"

"They made me be a judge for the All Scholastic Team. They changed it this year."

"They can change it if they want. When they hired you, did they say anything about coaching?"

"Yeah. They said that if I wanted the job, I'd have to agree to coach various after-school activities. I said yes. I didn't think I had a choice. I didn't know they meant athletics too."

I said, "Lots of school districts do this nowadays. It's getting harder and harder to find teachers to fill extracurricular positions. Now, before they hire you, they're sure to ask if you're willing to work outside your classroom. If you had said no, you probably wouldn't have gotten the job."

"I needed a paycheck. I had to say yes."

"Yeah, they can make you coach."

"But a gay guy being a coach? Come on."

"Come on what? You don't think there are gay coaches in sports?"

"Well, sure."

"So what's the problem?"

"They don't care that I'm in a locker room with a bunch of naked teenagers?"

"Are you going to be seducing them?"

"Teenagers aren't my thing."

"Good."

"How can I not look?"

"My suggestion is to avoid staring. They'll notice. Homophobia tends to run most strongly in exclusively male teenage groups."

"Do you think I should try and be completely in the closet, at least until I get tenure?"

"I can't make that kind of decision for you. How much do you think hiding your sexuality is worth to your psyche? What price are you willing to pay? You're right, I don't have to worry about making the rent like you do. You have my sympathy. My suggestion to you as a union official is— be a good teacher. Don't molest any kids and don't give anyone a reason to be suspicious of you."

"What do you mean don't do anything suspicious?"

I gave him the standard pitch any teacher would get— straight or gay, tenured or not. "Don't touch them for any reason. Don't be in a room alone with any student, male or female. If that happens, at the very least, make sure the classroom door is open."

"That sounds terrible."

"I'm surprised no one told you last year. Teachers have to be careful today. Probably kindergarten and first-grade teachers can touch the kids without suspicion, but not after that. It's too easy for some loony parent or child to make a wild accusation. It didn't use to be like that, but that's the way teaching is today."

"Thanks for the advice. I appreciate it." He smiled shyly

and asked, "Could I buy you a drink sometime up in Chicago?"

He had a great smile. I wondered if his shyness was an act or if this was another mode of seduction. I didn't know if he had planned the outfit and his presence here, or if it was really due to the "accident" of hearing people talking in the lounge. Maybe I'm too suspicious. I said, "I'm sure Scott and I could try to fit it into our schedule. Although, after he gets back, I expect his and my life will be hectic for quite a while."

His smile remained, but I thought I caught glimmers of worry and shyness in his eyes. He said, "Maybe just you and I could go?"

Back when I was dating, I never knew what to say to someone who I suspected was coming on to me, but who I didn't want to date. Certainly, Trevor might simply be a friendly guy making an innocent offer. As he grabbed the front of his shorts and readjusted himself, I thought—then again, maybe not. But I didn't want to give unclear messages either. As gently as I could, I said, "If you're asking for a date, I'm sorry, I love Scott and that is not possible. If you're being friendly, I appreciate it, and if the opportunity ever came up for the three of us to go, that would be fine."

He gave me a thin smile. "I understand."

But he didn't look look satisfied. If there was a nicer way to say no, I wasn't aware of it. I didn't need more distractions at this moment. I could have used less. With a cheery wave and passing closer to me than necessary, he left the room.

Celebrity seduction? My first groupie or a lonely gay guy who wanted to be friends? Scott talks about the people who hang around the baseball players. Male fans desperate for a touch of the magic. Female fans often eager for more. I think I was flattered more than annoyed. But I have been faithful to Scott since the day we met, as he has been to me, so Trevor wasn't even a remote possibility.

I hunted for any random custodian. I discovered most of them were at the new high school. Benjamin Harrison High was supposed to be ready to open in a few days. The population of River's Edge had more than doubled in the past few years, as had that of most of the southwestern suburbs of Chicago. It had taken them three tries, but they'd finally passed a bond referendum two years ago. In our district, they had expanded three existing schools, built two new grade schools, a junior high, and a high school. We'd also had a large increase in the number of teachers as well as a big turnover in personnel in general. In the past couple years, because of an early-retirement incentive program by the state and so many new kids, we had nearly a hundred new teachers out of a rapidly expanding staff of nearly three hundred.

The only person I found resembling a custodian was a scrawny teenager scrubbing floors on his hands and knees. Besides his youthful appearance, I could tell he was a teenager and not an adult by the numerous snarls he managed to work into his brief answers to my questions. There's no one like a teenager to communicate outrage at the world with tone of voice and body language.

I asked about people working in my room. He said, "I don't know nothing"—[snarl]—"about nobody"—[snarl]—"working nowhere."

"Do you know where the other custodians are?"

"I don't know where nobody else is. I ain't seen nobody."

I stopped in to see Jerome Blenkinsop, the other candidate for union president. He was packing boxes in his old classroom. He was going to be teaching in the new high school.

After we exchanged greetings, I pointed to the boxes. "I thought the janitors were supposed to do that."

"These are my personal things. They moved all the textbooks and cabinets."

Jerome was in his middle fifties. He wore designer jeans, cut off at the knees, and a plain white T-shirt that covered a slight paunch. His gray hair was three-quarter-inch long on top and short on the sides. He was around five feet six inches, round faced, with darkish circles under his eyes.

He dumped a few more things in a box, then said, "I'm concerned about the union election."

"I am too."

"Good. I think it's time for a new start and a new direction. I want to really stick it to the administration. For too long we've been afraid of confrontation."

"Where has Kurt been afraid of confrontation?"

Every teachers' union has a "radical faction." This was the group that always demanded war instead of negotiations. You could never possibly do everything that they wanted, because once you got them something, they wanted another thing. They lived for fighting and chaos. They were usually the most useless and most bothersome group to deal with.

Jerome said, "The most glaring example is last time when we gave up on that strike much too soon."

"Before we took the strike vote, you stood up at meeting after meeting and demanded we avoid striking. I remember you running up and down the halls talking to people trying to spread anxiety and fear. Most of the time

34

you didn't know the facts, but that didn't stop you from instigating uproar."

"I keep hearing rumors that Kurt has sold out to the administration."

"Who told you that?"

"I heard it around."

"If you can't give me specific names of who told you, then the accusation doesn't exist. I'd hesitate to accuse you of making it up." Actually, I wouldn't, but I was trying to be diplomatic while keeping my temper in check.

"Doesn't he have secret meetings with the administration?"

"What don't you think you are being told?"

"I think we have to be more strong and united."

"What does that mean?"

"And you told Beatrix Xury to quit the union."

"We're going to randomly skip from topic to topic without discussing any of them rationally?"

"What kind of loyalty is it to tell a member to just quit?"

"We're going to be taking loyalty oaths? Weren't you the one running around saying first-year teachers shouldn't join the union? I never did understand what put that harebrained idea into your head."

"You can't talk that way to a member."

"You mean to you or to Beatrix?"

"I want this to be like a real union where members can file grievances against each other. That would give us strength."

I know some unions do this. "It could make for bitterness and chaos."

"I don't want to fight with you."

"Yes, you do."

"You have no right to be mean to Beatrix."

"You know what she's like."

"She has a right to file a grievance."

"I told her that."

"That's not what she said," Jerome stated.

"I offered to help her fill out the paperwork."

"That's not enough."

"I'm willing to hold their hand through the process. I'm not willing to treat what should be an intelligent adult as if they were a moron."

"You can't be planning to endorse Seth. He and those elementary teachers will try and take over and run everything. They've been dragging down our salaries for years."

This was another problem with the school districts in Illinois. In most of the Chicago suburbs, the school districts usually had either all grade schools or only high schools. Teachers in districts with only elementary schools were the lowest paid. The unit districts, such as mine, the next highest. The solely high school districts paid the most. It was an odd system. Part of the reason for the disparity, I suspected, rested in the sexist notion that more elementary teachers were women and so "didn't need the money" since what they earned was supposedly a second income. An outdated notion, but one that no one had been able to dynamite out of existence. Many high school teachers in unit districts blamed the lower-grade teachers for keeping their salaries down. This did not make harmonious relationships between the staffs any easier.

I said, "Speaking of confrontation, have you gone to Seth to at least talk to him?"

"Why?"

"Strength and unity? Maybe you have common ground on which to work together."

"I haven't had the time." Which I took to mean that he didn't want to.

I asked, "Are you going to the PTA meeting tonight?"

"I think teachers, especially the union president, should be involved in all aspects of a community. Not only that, I've lived in River's Edge for years. It's a responsible thing to do. I'm going."

Kurt rarely attended anything but union meetings. This sure sounded like a slam on my friend. "Meaning Kurt was doing a poor job?"

"You just don't understand."

"What is it I don't understand?"

"You're Kurt's friend. I can't expect you to comprehend what I'm saying."

"I sure wish you made sense. I think you're just searching for an excuse to make trouble."

He went back to packing and ignored me. I left.

By the time I got to the library it was four o'clock. Meg was on the phone in her tiny office. She saw me and motioned me inside.

Into the phone she said, "Yes, Agnes, you have to be there. It's important. You know what these people are like. Look what happened to you." She listened for several moments, then said, "Great. Thanks, I'll see you there." She hung up.

"Marshaling the troops?"

"Yes."

"How is Agnes?" Agnes Davis had retired five years ago. She used to teach first grade in the district.

"This year she spent four weeks in South America looking for exotic birds."

"I remember she liked to take vacations to out-of-the-way and off-the-wall locations."

Agnes and Meg had been close friends for years. Before she retired, Agnes was famous for the parties she threw on the evening of every New Year's Day.

Meg said, "I've lived in this area a long time. I've called movers and shakers I've known in every group I can think of. People are concerned. More than a few teachers are going to be there."

"Maybe I should have helped make the calls."

"I don't think so. It looks better if you are on the sidelines. The issue should be who is the best leader for the PTA, not some right-wing political agenda. Belutha and her bunch will try and inflict their beliefs on all of us. However, there will be a crowd on the side of the angels there tonight. It will be dynamite. I hope Belutha tries something. I haven't been able to stand that woman since she proposed basing the library acquisitions budget on strict fundamentalist principles."

"What does that mean?"

"I'm not sure. Buying Bibles for every kid in the school? Who knows? She's a raving loony, so it could mean anything. She's been off her nut about filth in the library since she moved into the district in the early eighties. She hasn't gotten anything banned yet."

I remembered Meg telling me about some of the battles. "You still think I shouldn't go to the meeting?" I asked.

"Definitely not. It's going to be chaotic enough. If somebody has notified reporters, it could become a total circus. You want to be in the middle of that?"

"No. Especially not after this summer."

"You leave it in my capable hands."

I did trust Meg. I wasn't expecting her to fight my battles, but having her on my side was worth several tank divisions.

"Thanks," I said. "Call me after the meeting. I'll be up late tonight."

"Definitely."

"Something else I wanted to check with you. Do you know a guy named Trevor Thompson?"

"Second-year teacher, skinny, twenty-four, gay, teaches math, popular with the kids, does not have a lover, has the aura of a party person, thinks he's a stud. Other than that, no."

"He's worried about the meeting tonight. He thinks it might set off a gay witch-hunt and keep him from getting tenure. He was thinking about trying to hide in the closet to save his job." I described my encounter with him.

Meg said, "Perhaps he just wants to be friends."

"Possible. He didn't act studly so much. I'd put his actions in the category of blatantly offering himself. I don't need some twenty-something guy chasing me."

"The price of fame."

"I'm not ready for my close-up yet."

"He really thinks hiding in the closet is going to save his job?"

"I don't know. Some people get very frightened very quickly. I don't think I care much for Trevor. I know I don't want to be involved with him."

"If they go after the gay teachers, you may have no choice but to make common cause with him."

"I hope it doesn't come to that."

# 4

To get to my new home you take Interstate 80 west to the second exit past Interstate 55 and then go south. After my last home burned down, I brought fifty acres of prime farmland within an easy commute of work. I was out of Cook County now and in Grundy County. I'd picked the location because of its distance from any town. I enjoyed the peace and quiet. I love Chicago and Scott's penthouse on Lake Shore Drive, but for real living, give me a nice flat prairie and lots of space.

The house is a ranch style with three wings forming a U. The open end faces west with picture windows at the tip of each leg. I get a spectacular view of the sunset from numerous vantages. A center courtyard enclosed by the U had what was supposed to have been a flower garden. I took a course in basic plant how-to. Everything I planted died within a month. Finally, I'd rototilled the whole thing and planted grass seed. I thought in the future I might hire someone to put in a wooden deck.

The north wing has the master bedroom, library, and electronics center. The opposite wing has the kitchen, office, and guest rooms. The center core is a vast living room.

I furnished the new house carefully. Losing everything

in a fire is horrific, but it does give you a chance to start totally fresh assembling a household. The best example I can think of to illustrate my decorating style is my search for furniture. I was looking for a couch, so I became a denizen of every furniture store within fifty miles. I sat and/or laid on one davenport after another until I found the most comfortable one and then bought it. I used the same method for finding recliners, love seats, our king-sized bed, and other odds and ends. After picking out something, I would then tell the salesperson that I wanted items to match what I had just purchased. The result is I have clumps of furniture that match perfectly in juxtaposition with nearby groups that don't necessarily go together. On the other hand, nothing is extravagantly flashy, so nothing clashes horribly. However, my goal was achieved. All of it was immensely comfortable and based on what I wanted.

Sometimes I'd bring Scott with me on these buying excursions. He has less taste than I do, but his place has an organized-to-perfection look. That's because he cheated and hired a decorator to help him. This I refused to do.

For the walls, I picked out the posters or prints I liked the most and had them framed. Hanging in the library are my favorites of the moment—posters from the movies *Stonewall* and *Beautiful Thing*. I have on order an action shot of Scott pitching. He looks incredible with his muscles straining, crotch-cup bulging, full color, one of a kind. A friendly newspaper photographer gave me the original.

I had spent most of the last spring working on the design for the fields within two hundred yards of the house. With the help of various nursery personnel and landscape artists, I had planned carefully. I took great care to assure tons of shade for the house without blocking any of the view. By the time all the trees and bushes that were planted grow, it will look like a well-organized miniforest. Scott and I looked very butch in late winter and early spring, muffled to the eyes against the cold as we helped plant some of the flora.

I discovered the keys to a successful forest were don't overplant and have patience. The drive to the front door is going to be shaded by poplars and oaks that will meet overhead. Quite often I picked trees that bloomed most gloriously in spring—crab apples and dogwood—or that turned the most vibrant colors in fall—tupelos, sugar maple, hickory, along with stands of sassafras bushes.

One-third of the basement is a workout room. Before supper, I spent an hour down there using the new equipment Scott had bought me as a housewarming present.

A little after ten, Scott called from Seattle. He gave me the nightly report. "I did two sports-radio call-in shows and an early-morning television program. It is a good thing I've learned the answers and the questions by heart."

When I was with him, I had experienced the same phenomenon. The difficulty was the questions might be the same to us, but the answers were generally fresh to each audience that was listening.

I said, "You sound exhausted."

"I'm whipped. I walked out of another interview before it even started."

"What happened?"

"The usual."

From the first show we did, both he and I had refused to be on any program with a representative from the religious right or any other hate group. We made this clear before agreeing to be on any program. Three times, when we walked in, a host had said something like "By the way, I just happen to have so and so from . . ." And it would be some loon from an antigay group. The people on the programs were stunned when we reiterated our refusal and walked out. Neither Scott nor I were about to debate our rights, our sexuality, or our lives with anyone, much less some religious fanatic.

Scott continued, "What I'd really like to do is go off to our cabin up north. Better yet, I could buy us a home in the Vale of Kashmir, where no one knows us."

"I've got a phone message here from the *Kashmir Post-Gazette*. They want to interview you."

That got a small chuckle out of him. "I'd give my left nut to be in your arms right now." For the next few minutes, we were as tender and endearing to each other as any two people could be without being in each other's presence.

I felt a pleasant glow after the call. When he's gone on road trips in the summer, I like to stay up late reading. Perhaps the most relaxing thing in the world to me is having the window open late on a summer evening, lounging in oversized T-shirt, gym shorts, and sweat socks, my feet up, one lamp on in the whole house, sitting in my chair reading a book. The glorious silence interrupted perhaps by the rustle of the wind, or a distant train whistle, the rare swish of a car on the far-off road, accompanied by a night-bird or insect serenade. Capped off with a good book, it is totally perfect.

This time I picked up volume three of *A History of Private Life.*

At midnight I wondered briefly why Meg hadn't called. Certainly the meeting couldn't go that late.

I don't remember what time it was when I fell asleep in my easy chair with the book on my lap. I woke to the ringing of the phone. It was nearly 4 A.M. My first thoughts were that something terrible had happened to Scott or my mom and dad. I leapt up quickly. My book clattered to the floor.

When I picked up the receiver, the line crackled for several seconds. It sounded as if I were being called from a pay phone in a crowded bar on the far side of the moon. I said hello but got no answer. I was about to hang up when a muffled and distant voice came over the line.

"Tom Mason?"

"Who is this?"

"Agnes Davis. I was at the meeting tonight with Meg."

Then I heard nothing for several seconds, but finally Agnes's voice came through much clearer and louder. The background noises receded somewhat. Agnes sounded exhausted and frightened.

"I know you're Meg's closest friend. I've been trying to find out what they've done to her. She's been arrested for murder."

Someone in the background of where she was shouted, "Stop that, you son of a bitch." This was followed by several loud thumps and crashes.

"What's happened?" I asked.

"Jerome Blenkinsop is dead. Meg needs help. Can you get here?"

"Where are you, Agnes?"

"At a pay phone in the visitors' section of the River's Edge police station."

A deep, gruff voice shouted, "Hurry it up."

I heard Agnes answer, "Back off, you tub of goo."

I said, "I'll call a lawyer and be right there."

"Thank you. Try to hurry."

I hung up and dialed my lawyer. Todd Bristol was a good friend. He'd been my lawyer since before I met Scott.

Now we kept him on a yearly retainer. He was a partner in one of the big law firms on LaSalle Street in Chicago.

I woke him up and explained the situation. He'd met Meg and knew how close we were. He said he would drive out from the city immediately.

I changed clothes, grabbed my keys and wallet, and hurried to meet Agnes.

River's Edge is one of the oldest southwestern suburbs of Chicago, founded soon after Blue Island. From its outward appearance, you'd guess the police station was the first building erected after the founding. Across the street a new headquarters was under construction. The same population increase that had required new schools had forced them to build a new police station. Due to cost overruns, environmental lawsuits, weather delays, and bureaucratic snafus, it might not be finished until the middle of the next century. One forlorn, windowless wall was up. The builder seemed to have matched perfectly the dirty-yellow, grime-encrusted bricks of the original. Three of the mayor's opponents had filed a lawsuit accusing him of mismanagement of the construction.

Shattered glass, broken bottles, and rusted beer cans decorated the ground from the heaps of dirt near the new edifice to the unmown lawn and scraggly bushes around the old building. Inside, the first floor continued the ugliness scheme begun outside. Chips of paint peeled off the walls. Scratches and nicks beyond counting scored the solid-mahogany admitting counter. The smell of mold and mildew struck offensively. The windows were open, but no breeze stirred to relieve the beastly humidity. What had been pleasant at home amid the fields and trees became oppressive here in the confining enclosure. Five in the

46

morning felt as awful as high noon. Strips of tape with dead bugs clotted on them hung from the ceiling.

The few times I'd been in the station recently, the same cop seemed to be working the admitting desk. He saw me and carefully put down his paperback book *Total Blather* by Daisy Merdette. With loud grunts and groans suggesting he would die if forced to move faster than slow motion, he stood up, hitched his belt over his sixty-year-old paunch, and harrumphed over to the counter. Retirement had to be a day or two away. The only fan in evidence sat in the middle of his desk. It was small but aimed directly at his dry armpits.

I asked for Frank Murphy. He and I used to work together with whacked-out teens when he was in the juvenile division. He'd been in homicide the past few years. During that time we had seen much less of each other, but he was still a friend and the only contact I had in the department. I doubted if he'd be in at this hour, but it was worth a try.

Frank was not available, and I would not be able to see the prisoner. They were processing her. I desperately wanted to know what had happened. Meg was probably less than fifty feet away, and I couldn't speak to her.

Unable to see Meg, I said, "I'm looking for Agnes Davis, a friend of mine."

"She arrested too?"

"No. She's a mutual friend. She called me from here."

"We don't keep a record of friends' phone calls."

"Where do friends of arrested people usually make phone calls from?"

He pointed down a gloomy corridor.

I finally found Agnes in a waiting room with two pop machines that both had out-of-order signs. The dingy space smelled like burnt coffee. Two of the overhead lights blinked on and off at random intervals. Outside the pale, streaked window early gray dawn was breaking. We were the only ones in the waiting area. The rest of the friends of the criminals of River's Edge, like sensible people, were home in bed. As I walked into the humid holding room, Agnes stood up from a folding chair. She hugged me.

"Thank you," she said. "A million thank-yous."

In her early seventies, she was usually sprightly and lively. This morning her shoulders slumped, her hair was wildly askew, and every furrow on her face looked like a deep scar. We sat on a bench worn down by the butts of offenders for perhaps a hundred years.

"What happened?" I asked.

"Meg told me the story before the police arrested her. Blenkinsop got bashed with a *Smith's Comprehensive Encyclopedia.*"

"Why have they arrested Meg?"

"During the PTA meeting tonight, things were said and threats were made. Worse, they found her purse next to the dead body. Much worse, they have her fingerprints on the murder weapon."

"Can you give me all the details from the beginning?"

"Before the body was found, the evening had been awful. Afterward, there was chaos. For hours, police, school administrators and board members, teachers, parents, kids—just everybody—were running around."

My lawyer hurried into the room. Todd was tall and waspishly thin. He wore an impeccably cut, dark gray suit with a severely starched white shirt. If you used a microscope, you might find the faint red stripes in his dark gray tie. I'd only ever seen him dressed as if for court or a funeral. If I asked him about his attire, I knew he'd say that for a trip to the police station, it never hurt to look one's best. It might be impressive at the right moment. He wore glasses with thin gold rims. His sunken cheeks and crinkles around his eyes added to the impression he gave everyone that, with a few minor alterations, he could have been anyone's maiden aunt. He often sounded like it too.

I introduced him to Agnes.

"I've talked with several officials and a state's attorney," Todd said. "We're not going to be able to meet with Meg for a while. When that happens, they might only permit me in."

I explained about the meeting, then said, "Agnes was there. She might be able to give us information about what happened."

Todd took out a yellow legal pad from his briefcase and prepared to take notes.

"Where do I start?" Agnes asked.

Todd said, "Let's begin with all the details you can remember. Don't worry about not remembering everything. Take as much time as you need."

She filled Todd in on the background about the election, then began giving details about the meeting. "People spoke, shouted, argued. Nobody on their side made much sense. Your name came up, Tom."

"I don't care about that now. What's happening to Meg is what's important."

Agnes smiled briefly. She vigorously rubbed her eyes with her fists, then looked at us. "I'm more tired than I've ever been in my life. I've never had a friend arrested before. The police were terribly polite, but terribly firm. At first, Meg was too stunned to make much protest. When she got her wits about her and figured out she was a suspect, she began demanding a lawyer. They weren't quite so polite after that. Then they took her away."

"The meeting?" Todd prodded.

"If Belutha and her supporters used a shred of logic at the meeting, I didn't hear it. About the middle of the evening Meg told Belutha Muffin she could take her Neanderthal views and shove them up her butt. When she said that, people got very angry. I'm afraid what happened next was rather undignified but very funny. The silly cow, Belutha, finally lost that self-satisfied smile. She leapt across several chairs and charged Meg."

"Did Meg get hurt?"

"No, not by that awful person. She stood her ground. Before Belutha was finished crossing the distance between them, she was all red in the face and puffing harder than a hurricane. I thought she was just short of a stroke. Belutha may have been too exhausted for physical abuse by then, but she let loose verbal blasts that were equivalent to any tornado. Meg's comment when Belutha finally ran down was a deadly quiet and perfectly calm, 'Why don't you just die, you silly bitch?' I'm afraid that was the most controlled Meg was for quite a while."

I said, "I thought I was the one who had to work on keeping calm in overwrought situations."

Agnes chuckled. "Perhaps you can take lessons together. After she made that crack, several people got between them. Jerome Blenkinsop was one of them. They had to drag poor Belutha away. She swore she'd get even with Meg and her liberal librarian ways. Belutha never did get to make her little speech against you, Tom. She was escorted out and they called a recess.

"Later Jerome asked to speak with Meg privately. Meg motioned me to follow. I guess she wanted a witness. When we were a little apart from the others, Jerome went nuts. I had no idea he was one of Belutha's supporters. I was taken off guard and I think Meg was too. Emotions were running so high. Every time I turned around, someone seemed to be shouting. There weren't that many people nearby, but I'm afraid nearly everyone heard them. Jerome also ripped into you and your reputation. He was pretty angry you wouldn't support him in the election."

"If he was on Belutha's side, how could he have been interested in my support?"

"He was desperate to win. He called you several unpleasant names. At one point Jerome put his hand on Meg's elbow, but Meg yanked her arm away. What happened next is unclear. Someone claimed Jerome was pushed from behind. Whatever the cause, Jerome shoved Meg, who staggered back into me. Things became ugly. I'm afraid they both made threats they didn't mean. People got between them, and the incident ended.

"Everyone calmed down after that. When they resumed the meeting, their side suggested the elections be postponed because of all the turmoil. That got shouted down. Eventually, we voted. Belutha won by two votes."

I raised an eyebrow.

Agnes said, "The good guys lost. Happens more often than people care to admit. One of your strongest supporters did get elected vice president. It took a while to count the votes, but after they announced the results, the meeting began breaking up. Knots of people hung around discussing strategies, tactics, issues, and personalities.

"When we were ready to leave, Meg couldn't find her purse. She had stopped in the library earlier, but she knew she had it with her at the meeting because she had notes in it. She distinctly remembered taking them out before she went to the podium to speak. I don't recall seeing her with the purse, nor did I notice that she didn't have it.

"Because of the size of the crowd, we had the meeting in the gym. She even got a couple of custodians to pull out the bleachers and check under there. She began to think it had been stolen. Before making accusations, she figured she'd better check the library just to be sure it wasn't there. At that point, she went to the library, and I went to wait out by the car. The room had been stiflingly humid all night, and I wanted to get some fresh air.

"All the rest of this Meg told me while we waited for the police to arrive and before she got arrested. It took them forever to do their investigation.

"When she arrived in the library, she noticed several books were strewn on the floor down a nearby aisle. Meg's always very conscientious. She'd never leave a book out of place. She knew she hadn't done it, and that they hadn't been out of place earlier. She began a circuit of the perimeter of the room. Before she was a third of the way around, she saw a body. She realized right away it was Jerome. She didn't see him breathing."

Agnes drew a deep breath. "Meg was very subdued when she told me all this. I've never seen her so shaken. I would have been too. Finding a dead body has got to be the worst thing." She took a lace handkerchief out of her purse and dabbed at the film of moisture on her upper lip.

"What else did she say?" Todd prodded gently.

"That it was eerie. Her exact words were, 'I think of myself as cool, calm, and witty. I was none of those either at the meeting or at that moment.' I don't know how anybody could have been."

I said, "Those were more difficult circumstances than any of us ever want to be in."

Agnes wrapped her arms around herself, pulled in another deep breath, and resumed. "She didn't remember a conscious decision to act. She ran to the phone in her office, dialed 911, then locked up the room as tightly as possible. Then she began hunting for help. Everyone else was gone by that point except the janitors. She finally hurried out to where I was. We found the janitors together.

"I was there when she talked to the police initially. She told them the whole story including the part about hunting for her purse. That's important because they found it lying three feet from Jerome's body." Agnes sighed. "She had no idea how it got there. After she finished her story, the police began badgering her. I guess they found the purse pretty quickly. Others must have told them about what happened at the meeting."

"Did Meg remember seeing the purse when she saw the body?" Todd asked.

"She didn't think so. The police implied she'd dropped it in her confusion after the murder."

"If it wasn't there," Todd said, "then obviously someone got into the library after she left."

I said, "Or the murderer was still there watching her all the time."

Agnes shuddered. "This is more than a bit much."

"Who else has keys to the library?" Todd asked.

I said, "After all these years, I doubt if anybody really knows. Even without a key, access to any of our rooms isn't difficult. A flip with a credit card and you're in. Of course, the janitors would have keys."

"Can you give us a list of who else was at the meeting?" Todd asked.

"Usually less than ten show up. Tonight there were about twenty-five teachers and maybe seventy-five people from the community. I can try writing down some names for you later. Carolyn Blackburn, the school superintendent, was there, but she was talking to reporters for a short while afterwards and then left. Edwina skulked out before the reporters could get hold of her. Let me think." She paused for a moment. "Both candidates for union president were there as well as Beatrix Xury. She tried to make a statement about some field trip. She was mostly ignored. She got mad and left early. Meg pointed out to me somebody named Trevor Thompson, but I'm not sure who he was. A friend of yours, Tom, I think."

"I know who he is."

"He sat in the back and never said a word. Seth, the other candidate for union president, was there. He didn't say anything. I'm not sure I could remember everybody."

"Don't worry about it," Todd said. "The police can probably give us the names later. We've got to work on bail. Has she ever been arrested?"

"Not that I know of," I said.

Todd nodded. "I'll know more in an hour or two."

"I'm worried," Agnes said. "I know Meg didn't do it. It's just a matter of finding out who did or proving her innocence or both." She patted my arm. "You should be glad you weren't at that meeting. It was not pretty."

I said, "I'm going to do some investigating of my own. I'll call you if I find anything out."

She gave me another hug and left. I followed Todd back out front, then asked him, "Now what?"

"We aren't sure she wants me as her attorney. I'll get an answer to that and then I'll find out about a preliminary hearing. Bail for a murder charge isn't going to be cheap. Does she have the money?"

"If she doesn't, Scott and I do."

"Good to know. I'll work on it and get back to you. If what Agnes said about what the police have is accurate, they are starting with a strong case. Unless they happen upon another suspect, she is in deep trouble."

Todd left. By this time the day shift had come on duty. The person behind the reception desk might have been the same guy I saw earlier this morning or his identical twin. This time when I asked for Frank, I was told he was in.

I sat in Frank's office. He wore the same brown suit he wore 90 percent of the time. I don't know if he had just the one suit or whole racks full of brown suits that he kept in heaps on the floor so they'd all look equally rumpled.

He said, "I hear and see you're a big star now."

"Yeah, fame is as much fun as being run over by a tank."

"That happen to you often?"

"What?"

"That tank thing."

"Only this year. You should try being famous."

"No thanks."

"You heard Meg Swarthmore's been arrested?"

"Who is she?"

"Librarian at the school. A good friend of mine."

"I vaguely recall who she is. What'd she do?"

"Nothing. They think she killed Jerome Blenkinsop, one of the teachers."

"What evidence do they have?"

I told him about the purse, the fingerprints, and their dislike for each other.

"I don't know, Tom. It's not my case. I'll keep my ears open, but I can't do much for her or you."

"I'm going to ask people questions."

"Keep out of the way of the detectives. None of them are nearly as sweet as I am."

"Who could be?"

I knew he'd help me as best he could. If I went home, I

suspected I wouldn't be able to get any sleep. I was too concerned about Meg. I left and drove to the Frankfort Village Inn on La Grange Road in Frankfort to grab some breakfast, then hurried to school.

# 5

It was eight in the morning and only a few teachers, custodians, and administrators were around. I walked over to Carolyn Blackburn's office. Her personal secretary, Mavis Lukachevsky, announced me immediately.

Carolyn said, "It's awful about Meg."

"I was at the police station."

"How is she?"

"I couldn't get in to see her. My lawyer is working on getting her out on bail."

"I was too busy calming down raving board members and hysterical parents last night to get a clear idea of what happened. The police wouldn't tell me anything."

I gave her a brief outline based on what Agnes had told us. Carolyn shook her head. "I don't picture Meg killing anybody. Why would she need to? What's the point?"

"I know Meg didn't like Belutha. It seems Jerome was in Belutha's and Lydia Marquez's camp."

"That's news to me."

"Were you aware of any connection between those three?"

"I hear much less than people imagine. As superintendent I avoid gossip. Most of the time it is inaccurate or, worse, outright vicious lies. Sometimes it is better not to know. What you can ignore as superintendent can be fairly important. I can picture Meg doing in Belutha." She smiled briefly. "That actually might be amusing. I've seen them at meetings. Belutha tries to come across as sweetness and light, but there's a lot of anger there as well, which everyone finally saw last night."

"I'm going to be talking to a lot of people about the murder. I have to prove Meg innocent or find the one who did it."

"If I can help, let me know. Some of the folks who were at the meeting won't be eager to talk to you."

"I understand that. I know I can't make them open up."

"The police could get annoyed if they think you're interfering."

"I can handle that. Have you got time to tell me what happened last night?"

"Definitely. Do you know the outgoing president of the PTA, Louis Johnson?"

I shook my head.

"Well, at the beginning he ran the meeting. He didn't seem to know what he was doing and things got out of hand very quickly. It was supposed to be a candidates' forum. Questions were to be submitted from the audience and each candidate would answer them. First, they couldn't agree on who was going to screen the questions."

"Why did they need the questions screened?"

"Lydia Marquez suggested it. She made them do it the same way at the school board's candidates' night six months ago."

"Lydia was there last night?"

"In her glory."

"What did she say?"

"Let me tell this chronologically."

I nodded.

"They finally roped my secretary into screening the questions. She was very hesitant at first, but it turned out not to make much difference. To begin, each candidate was supposed to make an opening statement. Amelia Gregory, the other candidate for president, spoke first. She began a perfectly sensible speech about assuring cooperation between teachers, administrators, and parents. Before she could finish, Lydia stood up and began asking her a question about prayer in schools."

"This is a PTA issue?"

"It is to Lydia. Amelia looked confused. She tried to catch Louis's attention, but he ignored her. Mavis wasn't about to leap up and throttle Lydia. Several people in the audience shouted out demands that Amelia answer the question. Then several others began booing when they made those demands."

"Nobody tried to keep order?"

Carolyn told me that she'd finally taken control of the meeting. When she threatened to cancel the entire election, people began to get more reasonable. The plan was that when everyone was done speaking and both factions had been heard from, the candidates would still answer questions from the audience.

Carolyn said, "It was like holding a meeting in a simmering cauldron—waiting for it to boil. You were attacked once by name. Sometimes they used those phrases—'save the children' or 'endorsing a lifestyle'—but you weren't the real focus of the attacks or defenses. There were proposals for censorship and ending tenure. Prayer, I mentioned. One of the more difficult arguments for me to follow was the one demanding the PTA take a stand on abortion. It seemed like dozens of goofy proposals got made.

"What started the next fight was a person from Belutha's faction who sounded as if he was calling for a member of the Ku Klux Klan to be elected. As he spoke, I felt a prickle creep up my spine. Maybe he was one of those insane militia people. He didn't have much to say about the PTA election. He was more making a speech about his cause. He did everything but praise Hitler's Germany and call for the opening of concentration camps. I tried to cut him off, but he got abusive."

"Who was it?"

"Beorn Quigley. He teaches a few classes part-time in the industrial arts department. He didn't seem to be intimidated by my presence."

"He's obviously not worried about keeping his job."

"Meg had already made a statement, but after Quigley spoke, Meg elbowed her way to the speaker's podium. She barely controlled her fury as she spoke against everything he'd just said. She was nasty and vicious, but witty and clever as well. She was doing fine until she attacked Belutha by name. I don't think she should have done that. It caused a huge uproar."

"Agnes told me how Belutha charged Meg."

"I'm not sure Meg was all that innocent. However, I think even Belutha's most rabid supporters were appalled by Quigley. Meg dared Belutha or Lydia to refute what he'd said. Meg was practically challenging Belutha to start something."

"People have to take a stand at some point."

"Meg did that in spades. After I managed to reassert control, Jerome Blenkinsop, who had not said a word all night, stood up and defended Belutha and attacked Meg. I could see Meg was a little startled with an attack from that quarter. I called a halt to that—some employees still worry that a superintendent might get angry. Eventually, the two of them went off to some corner."

"Agnes said the fight continued."

"I was afraid of that."

"Do you remember who left the room after Belutha was helped out?"

"No. People were in and out and moving around. Throughout the meeting each side was trying to line up speakers. A few were making notes as others talked. Some huddled together in corners of the gym preparing their next statement. At the end everyone was sort of milling around as the voting took place and as we waited for the results to be announced. It would be nearly impossible to tell who was where when. I certainly don't remember Jerome walking out."

"Did you see Meg leave?"

"No."

"Who escorted Belutha out?"

Carolyn thought several moments. "I'm not sure. I was trying to get everyone else to settle down again. Sorry, that's all I remember."

As I got up to go, she said, "Last night you were defended vigorously. You have a lot of good friends and supporters in the community."

"I'm glad I wasn't the only topic of discussion."

"Belutha might have had a prepared diatribe against you, but she was escorted out before she could deliver it. As far as I'm concerned, you're a teacher in this district as long as you want to be."

"Thanks, I appreciate that. Right now I'm going to concentrate on finding the killer. Whatever happened at the meeting isn't important anymore. Getting Meg out is."

"But what happened earlier was important. Someone who was at that meeting is probably the killer. Good luck talking to people."

Before I left, she gave me a copy of the list she'd made of the people she remembered being at the meeting last night. She'd already given a copy to the police.

I returned to the high school complex to see who among the faculty was in the building. Georgette Constantine, the school secretary, met me at the office door. "This is awful about Meg," she began. "You're going to do something about it, aren't you?"

I like Georgette. She lives to fuss and fume. For years I bought her act as a major ditz, always befuddled, but willing to bend over backward to help you. It took a while, but I realized very little got past her at any time. She knew what and who to watch out for. Over the years, we'd become good friends, especially after I helped her organize the custodians and secretaries into their union.

I said, "I'm going to do everything I can to prove she didn't kill anybody."

"Even if she's found not guilty, they won't keep her on, will they? I'd miss having her around. She's so wonderful to work with. We've been friends for ages."

"I'm going to do everything I can to insure her continued employment here. Carolyn Blackburn didn't sound like she was ready to fire anybody."

"Good." She glanced around and then leaned closer. "I shouldn't be telling you this or showing you these." She held out some pink telephone message sheets. "These are for Edwina. There have been calls coming in this morning about you. They're saying they don't want their child in your classroom."

I riffled through them. There were six. I didn't recognize any of the names. "I haven't begun to memorize the names of the kids in my classes, but these don't sound familiar."

"I checked. Only one has a kid scheduled to be in one of your classes. Why would they call if they don't have students in your classes?"

"Fear? Ignorance? Outright stupidity? I don't know. How many more of these came in over the summer?"

She thought a moment. "Less than twenty-five here. I don't know about the district office."

"Carolyn didn't say anything about this."

"I talked to her secretary this morning. Parents are calling the district office as well."

It is always good to be in with the secretaries. They can tell you real information and be more truly helpful than anyone else in the school.

"There's something else," Georgette said. "There were two other calls besides these. These people were hateful. Before I could disconnect them, they became obscene and abusive. The second one started out more reasonable, but as soon as he started making threats, I hung up."

"Same person each time?"

"No."

"Male or female voice?"

"Male both times. Each sounded young. Not little kids, but at least teenagers. I'm certain they were not adults."

"If they were teens, their parents might have put them up to it."

"Are you in danger?"

"I hope not." I'd been with Scott in rural Georgia earlier

in the summer helping him with his father. The antigay prejudice there ran deep. I'd hoped for a little better in the Chicago area, but I knew there were crazies everywhere. "They didn't say anything specific?"

"No. Just threats, but I hung up before they could go very far."

"I'll be careful."

"The police are interviewing everyone down in the science office in the old section. The secretaries in each building have lists of people to call. We're helping the police find out who was at the meeting. Carolyn told the detectives we would cooperate any way we could. If you're careful, you'll be able to talk to any teachers right after they're done."

"I don't want to get the police irritated. Maybe I'll try that discreetly later on." I asked her about Beorn Quigley.

She frowned. "He's only part-time, so I don't see him much. I don't like him."

"Why not?"

"He's rude to me."

I knew this was enough to consign him to Georgette's seventh circle of hell. She promised to get me his phone number and home address and any other information she could. I thanked her and left.

I grabbed a stack of material from my mailbox. I glanced through it. Near the bottom was a flyer from Seth. It was a page dense with print. On the top was the slogan "Solidarity Forever." Kurt's and my names were in bold print in the text. I stood in the office and read it. Basically what was written accused both of us of incompetence, and if he was elected, Seth would put an end to rule by the high school teachers. I was seething before I was halfway to the corridor. This hadn't been in my mailbox late yesterday. I guessed this was a reaction to my refusal to back him. He must have written it quickly and placed copies in everyone's mailbox last night before he attended the PTA meeting. I didn't picture him doing it after he heard about the murder. What was the point?

I saw Trevor Thompson walk in the front door of the building. I swallowed my anger for the moment and hurried after him.

Today Trevor wore tight, white jeans, a blue T-shirt cut off at the midriff, and black running shoes. You've got to be fairly young and very slender to carry off white jeans and midriff shirts. Trevor was both. He looked decidedly sexy.

"I've got practice," he said before I could say anything. "I don't have time to talk."

"You were at the meeting last night."

"Listen, I'm really busy. I can't talk to you." He rushed off as if a group of rabid homophobes were after him.

His eagerness to talk to me had obviously been replaced by sheer terror. I wondered why and vowed to get an answer.

Celia Cosenza, the learning-disabilities teacher, came down the corridor. She looked as if she'd been crying. I worked a lot with Celia preparing for the difficult kids I would have in my classes each year.

"You okay?" I asked her.

"Jerome Blenkinsop was a good friend." She held a tissue to her nose and sniffed. "I can't believe he's dead, and I know Meg didn't kill him."

"Maybe you should be at home," I suggested.

"No. It's better that I come to work. I want to involve myself in something. I don't want to think about him being gone." She dabbed at her eyes. "How is Meg?"

"I'm not sure yet." I gave her a brief outline of my visit to the police station.

She said, "I don't know how anyone could think Meg did it. She is one of the nicest people around here. They've got the wrong person."

"I agree. How well did you know Jerome?"

"Each year, as with you, we talked about kids in his classes. We worked closely together for years." She sniffed again. "I can't think about him. I need to immerse myself in work. Do you have a few minutes? We've got to discuss these seniors that are going to be in your remedial reading class."

We did a student analysis every year before school started. These kids would have needs starting the first day of school, but I was anxious to do everything I could to help Meg. I told Celia this as gently as I knew how.

But she was persistent. "I have the class lists," she said. "If not now, when?"

Celia was a good person, and if a few minutes of rational work would help her, I could spare it. As we walked to her room, I told her about parents asking for kids to be taken out of my classes.

"You're so good with these kids. It would be a shame for these children not to have you for a teacher."

"I guess some of their parents don't see it that way."

"It's their loss. Let's presume the best. You're going to teach and have kids in class."

We spent thirty minutes examining the list of kids. When we finished, I asked, "Were you at the PTA meeting last night?"

"No. I had no business with the PTA last night. I've got a million kids to get ready for. I have to have daily plans for all of them. They've got to be in order for when school starts." She dabbed a tissue on her eyes again. "You know, I talked to Jerome as he was leaving school yesterday."

"Do you remember if he said anything significant?"

"He said he had a lot of people to see and that he felt obligated to attend the meeting. I thought about going. Maybe if I'd gone, Jerome would still be alive."

"Do you know his wife?"

"She's a good woman. They loved each other."

"Did you ever meet his kids?"

"No." She started to sniffle again. I tried to say some comforting words. When I left, she was pulling out a stack of forms.

I trudged down to my classroom. I wanted a few minutes to think and then begin my plan of attack. When I opened my classroom door, I stopped. Something was different. I walked farther into the room. Papers from yesterday still littered the desks and tables. They seemed to be in the same order I had left them. It was remotely possible that the janitors had been in to sweep up. I checked the floor. Stray bits of packing material still clung to the tiles. Even with the marginally competent crew we had, they would have gotten these scraps with the most perfunctory cleaning. The custodians hadn't been in.

I sat in the chair behind my desk and carefully looked at each item in my view. Then it struck me. Yesterday, all the textbooks resting flat on their sides on the shelves had had the open end facing toward the door. Now they all faced the window. What earthly purpose did it serve to change the books? I took several off each shelf and looked behind them. Nothing.

I shrugged off the feeling of uneasiness. Before I left, I checked everything else carefully. The computer was intact and undisturbed. I was most concerned about my union files. I take notes at every meeting I have as union building representative. As grievance person, I'd kept a file on every complaint I'd received. The originals of all these were at home, but I kept copies of everything in school. I'd lost several years' worth of originals in my fire. None of the cabinets in this old section had locks that locked securely. My classroom doors, like the library's, were easy enough to break into with any kind of hard edge.

I systematically checked all the files. I thought several might have been tampered with. I don't memorize every piece of paper that goes into each folder, but I do have a system. I always save my notes from each time I talk to a teacher or administrator in chronological order. In several folders these were slightly out of order. One of these was Beatrix's. Another a first-year teacher who couldn't control her classes. I couldn't swear in court that the problem wasn't simply that I had misfiled these.

I wasn't sure what the new placement of the textbooks or the disturbed files meant, but I was determined to get to the bottom of both problems. I also needed to find out if they were connected to the missing plan book yesterday.

# 6

I drove to Zachary Taylor Elementary School to find Seth
O'Brien, author of the nasty diatribe. I found him sitting at
his desk, writing on a sheet of legal-size paper. He wore
baggy shorts and a T-shirt that reached to midthigh. His
room was decorated with cheery, bright posters of cuddly
animals, and the alphabet marched across the top of the
front of the room—white letters on a green background.
One bulletin board had a smiling Mr. and Ms. Times-Tables.
He looked up as I walked in.

I said, "I saw your flyer about the election." I held it up
in my hand. "What did you do, talk to me then run to your
computer? You might have waited. I hadn't talked to your
opponent yet."

"I knew you weren't going to support me. I saw no reason to wait. I put the notes in the high school mailboxes
last night, before the meeting, and in the elementary
schools early this morning. I thought of taking them out of
the mailboxes after I heard about last night's unfortunate
incident, but it was too late by then. People had started to
read them. Anyway, they aren't about Jerome."

"You don't think it was a little harsh?"

"I don't know what you're talking about. I don't like

your tone. You don't sound very professional. Why are you taking this so personally?"

"You print and distribute a personal attack on me, and you accuse me of being unprofessional? You don't expect me to take a personal attack personally? Are you nuts?"

"This is just the kind of thing I was talking about. You're being much too confrontational. So has Kurt and the union."

"You mean, you get to say something outrageous, untrue, and totally stupid, but if I say anything, I'm confrontational? Do you have the slightest logic circuit in your brain?"

"Why should I bother to fight with you? I'm going to win the election now."

"How convenient for you."

"How dare you? The police are at the high school. They're trying to get everyone who was at last night's meeting rounded up to interrogate. If I hadn't been running for union president, I wouldn't have been involved in any of this. I wish I hadn't gone to the meeting last night. I didn't ask for any of this."

"You don't sound heartbroken about Jerome's death."

"It's a horrible thing. How can you presume I'm not upset about his death? I taught in the same district as he."

"I thought you said you weren't going to the meeting."

"I changed my mind."

"Where were you after the meeting last night?"

"I beg your pardon?"

"What time did you leave? Did anybody see you go?"

"Did I miss something? Are you on the River's Edge Police Department?"

"Not yet."

"Nor will you ever be."

"My friend is accused of murder."

"You want to be an amateur sleuth? Please, leave that Jessica Fletcher crap alone. I'm not answering any of your questions."

An unpleasant impasse if I ever heard one.

He got up from his desk and walked toward the door.

"You're just walking out?"

"I'm going to the bathroom."

"In the middle of a conversation?"

He simply left.

I hunted down the new head custodian in the district, Robert Tusher. He was a short, roly-poly man. All the custodians wore brown uniform pants with a brown work shirt. Probably from the same company that made Frank Murphy's suits. I asked if anybody had been in my room this morning.

"You're the guy from TV talk shows with the baseball player?"

"Yeah."

"Your room in the west wing of the old high school?"

"Yes."

He thought a minute. "Wasn't supposed to be anybody in there. Except for a couple community service kids, we were all over at the new school getting it ready for the big meeting Friday. We're setting up tables and chairs in all kinds of different places. Those community service kids don't do the slightest thing more than what they are told. You've got to watch them every minute."

I believed that.

He gave me more details than I needed for the next few minutes about opening the new building, difficulties with teenagers on probation, and impossible teachers. I let him talk. It's always a bright idea to keep on the good side of a custodian. After the school secretaries, they are the most powerful people in a school. He finished, "Didn't you have some kind of trouble yesterday afternoon?"

"You heard about that?"

"My staff has to report any problems to me at the end of the day. One of the kids said you talked to him."

A snarling but loquacious teenager. I asked, "Which of your people were on duty last night?"

"I heard Meg Swarthmore is a friend of yours. You worried about her being accused of murder?"

"Yeah."

"I already talked to the cops. They've cleared my people. They were in each other's presence the whole night."

"They went to the john together?" I asked.

"My folks vouch for each other. Do you have somebody to give you an alibi?"

"I was home."

"Alone?"

"Yes."

"I was with my wife. Sounds like you've got more to worry about than I do." He walked away.

Working with the list I had gotten from Carolyn, I returned to the high school and went in search of people to question.

First, I stopped outside the library. The light inside came from several skylights they'd installed in the roof in the past year. Warm sunlight flooded the room. Police barrier tape covered all the entrances. I had to do all my observing from the doors. I could see nothing of significance from my vantage point.

At the entrance to the old wing, I saw a few people sitting in folding chairs outside the science office. These must be people waiting to be interviewed. A young cop near the door said to me, "Can I help you, sir?"

"I wanted to talk to a few people."

"Were you at the PTA meeting last night?"

"No."

"Then if you could leave, sir, that would be a help to the police."

There was no point in crossing her. I retreated. The school was starting to heat up in all its unair-conditioned splendor. I supposed I could simply wait around the corner for people to come by.

Lydia Marquez came trundling down the corridor toward me. Not often in our lives do we get to see evil incarnate walking toward us. Lydia was probably in her early forties. She did not have horns, a tail, and cloven feet. She was in a sleeveless rayon shirt that revealed mounds of flesh best left covered. If the overstuffed-sausage-casing look ever became fashion law, she'd certainly dwarf the competition. Her jeans were baggy enough to cover the bulges of the back end of a rhinoceros. The pant legs billowed around her, making her resemble somewhat a tent on legs. Her fat butt jutted out behind her. She had a downcast look. Her look said even if a busload of comedians showed up at her house, she'd be too tired to laugh. If there was a street, I'd have walked across it to avoid her.

I didn't have to worry about whether to approach her or not. Once she made eye contact with me, she marched over and planted herself directly in front of me.

She introduced herself, then said, "I've heard so much about you, but then who in the district hasn't?"

"I'd rather be loved than famous. Didn't somebody say that?"

"There's something I don't understand about you."

"What's that?"

"What I don't get is if all the running around and arguing and fighting is all worth it."

"It's worth it for Meg. We're more than good friends."

"No, I meant with all these television shows. It certainly can't be fun."

"I don't define my life by doing only that which is fun."

"Maybe I didn't say that well. There's got to have been an enormous emotional toll on you. Is it worth it? Is the price you're paying in emotional health, psychic strength, loss of sleep, physical and emotional exhaustion, worth what you are getting out of it?"

This was almost more nasty than a melodramatic confrontation. At least then I could make sarcastic and witty cracks while she prattled on like an imbecile. Now she was coming across almost as someone who cared that I lived and breathed. Now I was being melodramatic.

She concluded, "For a choice you made, you are suffering a great deal."

"The choice I'm making is to stand up to people like you."

"You know, you really aren't very important."

"Pardon me?"

"You may have been on television, and you may have tenure, but in the larger scheme of things, you aren't very significant."

"How kind of you to point that out to me."

"Retribution will be exacted."

"By whom? You? For what?"

"I may not be the instrument. God will decide."

"How nice for him or her."

"Blasphemer."

"I guess."

She pointed a finger with a large turquoise ring on it at me. "I'm a school board member here. You have to treat me with respect."

"No, I don't. Respect isn't something just conferred on someone because they get a few more votes than someone else. Just think Richard Nixon, and you'll get the point."

Her jaw twisted at an odd angle. A vein in her forehead seemed about ready to pop. I wondered if causing someone to have a stroke was actionable. While she was deciding whether to explode or not, I asked, "What time did you leave the meeting last night?"

She began walking away. "You'll be sorry."

This was the second person in less than an hour to just up and leave. I wondered if this was the new "mature person's response" to stress. Certainly I could put her in the lifelong-enemy category.

In the teachers' lounge, I found two people, heads together and laughing hysterically. When I walked in, they greeted me warmly.

Rachel Seebach, a member of the English department, said, "You should have been at the meeting last night. I'd like to have bust a gut laughing. Meg was hysterical."

"You were both at the meeting?"

They nodded.

Rachel was in her midtwenties. She wore casual shorts and a Harvard University T-shirt. From the grime and dust on her hands, I presumed she'd been unpacking textbooks in her room. Rachel was fun to sit next to at department meetings. She had plenty of sarcastic comments to share under her breath. The funniest times were when she would make a joke, I would laugh, and she would sit stony-faced as if she had nothing to do with my roaring mirth.

I said, "Meg's been arrested for murder."

"We know," Rachel said. "That's part of what is so funny. I can maybe picture Meg slowly reading someone to death, but not bopping them over the head."

"Everybody knows how it happened?"

"I heard it was the *Oxford English Dictionary*. The abridged, one-volume edition." This comment was from Jim Geraghty, another member of the department. A good-looking man, he spent a great deal of time campaigning to be English department chair. He was pleasant enough and usually on my side in interdepartmental squabbles.

"You guys aren't sorry Jerome's dead?"

"Are you?" Jim asked.

"I worked with him a few times with the union."

"I'm sad about him dying," Rachel said, "but it's like at a wake, especially when you didn't know the person. Laughter helps sometimes, and Meg was so funny last night."

I put some quarters in the pop machine, got a soda, and sat down at their table.

I said, "I wish I'd been there. What happened?"

"Well," Rachel began, "first one of those religious-right people got up and said we should start the meeting with a prayer and saying the Pledge of Allegiance."

Jim continued, "Louis Johnson just gave a weak smile and said he guessed it would be okay. Before anybody could object or say something intelligent, there we all were standing up praying and pledging."

"Louis is a waste of good breathable air," Rachel said. "Before Amelia Gregory could get halfway through her opening statement, Lydia Marquez stood up and said she had a point of order. Poor old Louis never had a chance. Before long both sides were shouting to be heard. Carolyn

Blackburn finally took control. That helped keep things sane, but it didn't keep people from saying some pretty nasty stuff."

Jim put in, "While Meg was giving her talk at the lectern, one of them walked up with a Bible and waved it in front of her. All Meg said was, 'It would help some if you were literate enough to read that.'"

"Did anyone see Jerome leave?"

"We've been trying to figure that out," Jim said. "Each of us has been in to talk to the cops. They told us not to discuss it among ourselves, but this is the biggest thing to happen in the school in ages. We're curious too."

"As near as we can figure," Rachel said, "he left about the time the voting began."

Jim nodded. He added, "We know for sure he didn't come back and wasn't there for the announcement of the results."

"They talked about you a little," Rachel said.

"That didn't get far," Jim said. "They can't just take off after a teacher at some PTA meeting. A lot of the teachers lined up to talk after that. Their side could barely get a word in edgewise. We've got to protect our own."

"Who left when?"

"Hard to remember," Rachel said. "Louis Johnson announced the vote so he was there at the end. A lot of people were still around. There wasn't an organized exodus."

I said, "The police must be keeping a huge chart on who was where when."

"Maybe not," Rachel said. "They've got their suspect. When they talked to me, they seemed to be more interested in confirming what they already knew. If I were you, I'd be suspicious of everyone."

Jim said, "To save you the embarrassment of asking,

Rachel and I left the meeting together. We stopped at Oleantha's Sports Bar in Orland to get something to eat. We left about midnight."

"Thanks."

Rachel said, "What's really tough to figure is, who comes under more suspicion? Those who left or those who stayed?"

I said, "If they left the room before Jerome, they could have simply waited for him and lured him away. If they left after him, they might have caught up with him. Either way the killer could have come back to the room afterward and no one would have been the wiser. They'd never be able to pin the time of death down that closely so that a minute-by-minute analysis of movements is going to help."

"Does anybody know why Jerome left the room?" Rachel asked.

"He could have simply been going to the bathroom," Jim said.

"There are washrooms between the gym and the library," I said. "He had to be going out of his way and there had to be a reason. Maybe he was meeting someone."

"Trysting in the library stacks," Jim said. "You'll be disappointed to know that nobody came to the meeting covered in blood and gore. I'd have noticed. Nobody acted suspicious."

Rachel asked, "How is Meg holding up?"

"I haven't been able to talk to her." I needed to call Todd and check on his progress with getting Meg bail.

Jim asked, "What was it like being on those television shows?"

"More exhausting than I ever thought it would be."

Beatrix Xury burst into the room. "Isn't it awful about

Meg and Jerome," she gasped. She stood in front of me holding a calibrated thermometer in her hand.

We all nodded and murmured at her.

"I can't believe something like this would happen in our district. Can you imagine? Are any of us safe? Are they going to take action to protect us?"

"I hadn't thought to ask," I said.

"Well, you should. There's a murderer on the loose. You've got to do something."

"I'm going to prove Meg innocent."

Beatrix rounded on me and held out the thermometer. "I presume you're going to file a grievance about the lack of air-conditioning. I just checked seventeen different rooms. Mine is over eighty-nine degrees."

Jim said, "I sure wish the union could do something about the heat. It's going to be miserable with these kids in here. Most of the faculty are bringing fans from home. How can kids learn anything with the heat engulfing them? It's like trying to teach underwater."

Rachel added, "Can't you do something?"

"They won't let us take them outside anymore," Jim said.

"Yes," Rachel said. "One parent complained last year that her child wasn't learning because they took them outside one day for one class period."

One parent complaining in the River's Edge school district was enough to start an avalanche of administrative panic.

"What are you going to do?" Beatrix demanded. She looked triumphant. Finally, she'd picked an issue that would have broad public support.

"If you don't get satisfaction from the administration,

you should call the Occupational Safety and Health Administration," Rachel suggested. "They can file suit and make them fix the air-conditioning."

Everybody always wants to help.

I said, "They can investigate. If the administration can show they're making a good-faith effort to fix things, OSHA won't do anything."

"Is the administration trying to fix this?" Beatrix asked. "I don't think so. You'll have to do something. It isn't just me complaining. Everybody is upset."

"I'll get on it," I said.

"It's about time."

"Beatrix, what time did you leave the PTA meeting last night?" I asked.

"I left early. No one was interested in listening to me. I went to the hardware store to buy this thermometer."

"Anybody see you leave?"

"I don't need to check my movements with anyone. You will find the time on my receipt from the hardware store. Then I went home. I've told you and the police as much as I wish to about the meeting."

Beatrix stalked out.

Rachel said, "In the 'Moron Olympics,' Beatrix would win all the gold medals. That woman needs a personality transplant."

I said, "She'd probably get a donor who was a serial killer."

"We'd be better off," Rachel responded.

"Sure wish you could do something about the air-conditioning," Jim said. "My room is in that odd corner between the old and new wings. It is totally ghastly."

That was one of the main things about being a union official. There was always another person with a new problem to be solved immediately. I went in search of heat relief and suspects.

I stopped in the office. Georgette wasn't in. Edwina was going through some files on the counter. She wore black horn-rimmed glasses and a pantsuit the color of a *caffè latte,* heavy on the cream.

I said, "Can we fix the air-conditioning?"

"Fat chance." Her attitude toward me was kind of weird—at times flippantly sarcastic as if she were willing to dare me to try to get something changed.

I asked, "Can you say OSHA?"

"You wouldn't."

"I would and can."

She shook her head. "We're doing everything we can."

"When did that start? I heard it wasn't going to be fixed."

"Five minutes before you came in."

"I'd like you to have to work in the heat like the rest of us. I bet if your office was miserably hot, it would get fixed."

She smiled at me. "Feel the atmosphere in here? It did get fixed. We'll get on your complaint right away."

I walked out. Edwina was good at telling lies to your face. There must be a course on the graduate level called Bald-Faced Lying for Administrators. I had no doubt Edwina had gotten an A.

I used the phone in the English office to try to find out Meg's status. Frank Murphy wasn't in. Todd's secretary said he was still in River's Edge. There was no answer at Meg's. Out of perversity, I decided not to call OSHA right then. I know it's immature, but I felt hard-pressed, and not calling immediately was my little way of rebelling. As if it made some kind of big-deal difference.

In the corridor near the line of people waiting to be questioned by the police, I spotted Mavis Lukachevsky. She beckoned me over. I followed as she led me into an empty classroom.

"What's up, Mavis?" I asked.

"Georgette gave me the address of Beorn Quigley, that man at the meeting dressed in the battle fatigues." She handed me a slip of paper with a name and address on it.

"Thanks."

"He really frightened me. I think he was armed."

"A concealed weapon?"

"If anyone would have one, he would."

I examined the paper she gave me. "He's the owner of a feed store?"

"Yes. He comes from a very prominent family. They've lived in the district a long time."

She handed me a file folder with several pages of copies in it.

"What's this?"

"Georgette told me I should give them to you. She said you would never tell the superintendent."

"Carolyn won't find out from me. Thanks for your help."

"Thank Georgette. Not only are all the secretaries making the calls we're supposed to make, we're finding out information and passing it on to her. She likes Meg and you a lot. You're nicer than the other union people who call the district office. You're polite and never make impossible demands."

Mavis glanced over her shoulder and saw Edwina looking at us through the glass in the office. Mavis moved her head slightly in Edwina's direction. "Anybody asks, I gave you the health files you requested on kids you're going to have in your classes."

I looked in the folder. Under the first few documents there were health notices. Always tell as much of the truth as you can. It is important to get health information on the students you're going to teach. If a kid has some special health need, and you ignore it because you didn't read the proper health notices, you might be held liable. Georgette would have been bright enough to know this and planned ahead for a cover for the file.

Mavis left and I walked to my room to read through the data. Quigley had a child in third grade, another a freshman in high school, and an older child in a private college in Montana. The River's Edge Feed Store he owned was on Route 6 on the way to Joliet. I decided to take a trip out. It was daylight, and in a public store, I didn't think he could get violent. If there was no one else there, I could just turn around and walk out.

It was nearly noon and I was feeling the lack of sleep. I stopped for several small bottles of orange juice at a convenience store on 159th Street and Wolf Road.

The store Quigley worked at was the only unboarded-up one in a small strip mall. The parking lot had two pickup trucks parked outside. I crossed the gravel surface and entered the store. The room was dusty and smelled of manure. The property turned out to be far more extensive than it looked from the front. Out in back stood numerous tin-roofed sheds filled with row upon row of bags of seed, feed, and fertilizer.

One man wearing gray steel-rimmed glasses stood behind the counter. He was in his early forties: tall with broad, round shoulders, a ring through his left nostril, and blond hair cut severely short. He was talking to a man in his late teens. This guy wore dusty blue jeans, a white

T-shirt with a beer-company logo, and cowboy boots. As I approached, I heard them talking about the possibility of rain. Out back I could see another man maybe in his late twenties. He was strolling down the aisles looking down at the bundles and bags.

The man behind the counter nodded at me. He finished his conversation with the young man and rang up his purchases. The youth called to the other man, and they left.

He turned to me. "Can I help you?"

"Are you Beorn Quigley?"

"Yeah. Who's asking?"

"Tom Mason. I'm a teacher at Grover Cleveland High School. There was a murder at the school last night. You spoke at the PTA meeting."

"I sure did. I know who you are now. I haven't seen you on television, but I know your name."

"How come you went to the meeting?"

"I live in River's Edge and teach part-time at the school. What happens there concerns me. People have to speak up for what they believe in. Local elections are what's important. That's where the real direct effect on our lives is. I keep trying to convince my friends that they have to pay more attention to who's in charge locally. They're the ones who raise our taxes."

"I was told you made a lot of strong statements."

"My beliefs are based on the Bible and common sense."

"What beliefs are those?"

"Less government intrusion in our lives, less taxes, less welfare, less giveaways, the government being given back to the people."

I was tempted to ask, which part of the Bible are those in? Did I want a debate or did I want to solve the murder? Did I really care that much what he believed?

"What time did you leave the meeting last night?"

"Precisely seven minutes after ten. They had just announced the results of the election. I was pleased. I walked out with three friends. Would you like me to get them together to talk to you?"

"Not really, but the police will have to check it out."

"I can handle that."

I was sure he could. I left.

# 7

Back at school, I walked out to football practice. Trevor had his arm around a kid in a football uniform. The athlete was sitting on a bench. As I got closer, I saw the kid was bent over and holding his knee. He was moaning softly. I heard the sound of a siren, and a few moments later an ambulance pulled up. Behind it was a brown Chrysler. These contained medical personnel and parents respectively. The coach of the team, Jack Palmer, hurried over. He'd been promoted to head coach when Kurt gave up the job after his heart attack.

The paramedics briefly examined the teenager.

"Is it broken?" the kid asked.

"We're going to get you to a hospital where they can take X rays." They put him on a stretcher and took him away.

The rest of the team had gathered around to watch. Palmer told them to take a five-minute fluid break. Team managers rushed to vats of soft drinks and began distributing bottles.

The heat was oppressive. The sun beat down on the field. I remembered my own playing days and for a few seconds wondered how I could have been so oblivious to the misery. Watching the team move quickly in the heat reminded me of the answer. It was fun and I was young and I didn't care. At the time, playing football was all that mattered.

Palmer gave me a friendly greeting. Two years ago, as building rep, I'd helped him with some problems he'd been having with his family insurance through the school.

Palmer nodded toward the departing ambulance. "That was my starting quarterback. I think his knee is shattered. Whether it is or not, my guess is this was his last day out here." He shook his head. "Nothing you can do about that kind of thing. It was a clean tackle. The kid who did it is in tears in the locker room. He's lucky. He'll probably survive to play again." He sighed. "What can I do for you?"

"You heard about Jerome and Meg?"

"Yeah. Who hasn't?"

Trevor stood up to leave.

"I wanted to talk to one of your assistants." I pointed at Trevor.

"Sure, I can spare him. Everything's pretty organized. The administration keeps giving us these people who don't know anything about sports."

Trevor looked irritated at this.

"Can you do something about that?" Palmer asked.

"You know the answer, Jack, we've gone over it before. They have the right of assignment and transfer over all coaching positions."

"Doesn't seem right."

Every district I knew posted all extracurricular duties each year. This meant any teacher could apply for any of those after-hours jobs. So a coach of twenty years could be out the next season, and the administration was not required to give a reason. This made for a situation ripe for complaints and grievances. All of which the union would lose. Lots of people did get the coaching job they wanted or had had for years, but districts both liked to keep control and have the ability to get rid of incompetent coaches.

"This won't take long," I said.

Jack left.

"What?" Trevor snarled.

"You turning into a teenager?"

"Just tell me what you want and let's get this over with."

"How come yesterday you're eager to chat and now you don't want to be near me?"

"Are you stupid?"

"I'm not sure I'm in your league. Perhaps you could give me lessons."

He turned red. "I shouldn't have said that, but don't you see? If I'm friends with you, they might think I'm gay."

"They who?"

"People. Everybody. The kids."

"Everybody who talks to me and all my friends are gay?"

"You know what I mean."

"Actually, I don't."

"What is it you want?"

"All I want to know is when you left the meeting last night."

"I don't remember the exact time. It was before the voting. I was bored so I left early. I drove to a gay bar in the western suburbs. I met a couple friends. We had a few drinks and played a little pool."

"You going to tell the police this?"

"What do you mean?"

"They haven't talked to you?"

"I'm supposed to go after practice. They had a lot of people in line."

"They're going to want to know the answers to my questions."

"I can't tell them I went to a gay bar."

"Why do you have to identify it by sexual orientation?"

"Will my friends be questioned?"

"Maybe. Did you know Jerome?"

"We were in the same department. I saw him at meetings. I don't hang around school much. Lots of the teachers think of this as a social place, but other than you, I don't know any gay people here. I didn't find out about you until this summer, and you're not interested in going out. I usually party only with gay people."

"Did you ever have any disagreements with Jerome?"

"No."

"Who were you supporting in the union election?"

"I really didn't care who won. I'm not interested in that union stuff. Not many of the new teachers are."

This was true. If you went to a union meeting, and this didn't apply to just teachers' unions, most of the time you only found people over forty.

"Yesterday, you were concerned about your job," I said.

"And killing Jerome is going to insure that I get tenure?"

"Probably not. Did you kill him?"

"Get serious. I barely knew him. I had no reason to. No, I didn't."

"Did you notice if Jerome was still at the meeting when you left?"

"Look, I noticed myself and nobody else. I gotta get

back to looking like an idiot out here." He began trotting away. He got about ten feet, then turned abruptly. "Can I get sued for this kid getting hurt?"

"Were you negligent?"

"I was in charge of their group when it happened." He took a step or two back toward me. "I don't think I did anything wrong."

"The district has insurance and you're covered through the union as well. It's not time to worry about that."

He nodded. "Thanks." He hurried away.

It didn't surprise me that he was afraid of being sued. Teachers worry about that a lot these days. I was surprised at Trevor's gay avoidance. I thought young gay guys weren't as paranoid about being found out as I had been when I started teaching. When you're gay, a certain general wariness about the world is natural, but Trevor was as self-hating and paranoid as the worst closet queen in the fifties. I had some sympathy with him from my own history, but this much paranoia seemed way out of line. Plus, he'd known I was gay yesterday when he wanted to be friends. Something didn't add up here.

Back in school, I stopped at the office. Georgette said I had several messages. One was from Todd. Meg would probably get bail tomorrow.

I called his office.

"How is she?" I asked.

"Very depressed. She said she didn't want to see anyone. So, if you're planning to go over, don't."

"I think she'd see me. We're close friends. Why wouldn't she?"

"I'm not sure. Most people get really depressed when something like this happens. No matter how innocent you are, or as bubbly as you've said Meg is, eventually it dawns on you that you could be convicted and spend significant amounts of time in jail. All the stories lately about people falsely convicted and stuck in prison for years don't help. She's scared. Does she have family in this area?"

"No. An ex-husband in downstate Illinois. She never had kids."

"You might plan to come to the hearing. Maybe by then she'll see the wisdom of having friends around for support. Going it alone at a time like this is tough. You also might want to arrange for money at that time."

"How much?"

"Bail will be at least a hundred thousand. So you need to bring at least ten percent—ten thousand." He explained the process to me and we hung up.

Another message was from Scott. He would be in around six o'clock and would hire a limousine to take himself out to my place. He always insisted on my not picking him up or taking him to the airport. The limousine service was easier and he could afford it. O'Hare traffic at six in the afternoon on any day could be a nightmare.

I was tired and hungry. It was nearly three o'clock. Before I left, Georgette said, "You have a call from Agnes Davis. She doesn't want you to call her, but she gave me her address. She hopes you have time to stop by this afternoon around four." She handed me a sheet of paper.

I thanked her for all her help, then stopped in my classroom. This time, nothing seemed odd or out of place. At first. Then I couldn't find my notes that I'd been constructing for the start-of-school list of things to do. No one was in the corridor. The nearest custodian I found claimed not to have seen anyone going into or out of my room. I called down to the office on the intercom and asked Georgette if she knew about anybody who'd been looking for me or who might have had an excuse to enter my room. She said no. I began to feel uneasy. I knew those notes had been nowhere else but in the middle of the top drawer of my desk.

I was too tired to continue puzzling about the anomaly. Staring at the empty space in the middle of my desk wasn't going to make the papers reappear. Nor was it going to make whoever was doing this pop out of the cabinet and confess.

I used the phone in the English office to call OSHA about the air-conditioning. The person there was actually pretty nice, nor did he give me unrealistic hopes. He would send me the proper form. His main concern was my willingness to follow through on a complaint.

"You are going to stick with this?" he asked numerous times.

"It's an impossible situation," I said.

"We get too many people who get scared off and back out."

"I'll stay with it. I'm the union rep here so I'm in for the duration. What if they solve it while I'm in the process of filling out forms?"

"You can be happy."

I returned to my work in my room. By the time I had to leave for my four o'clock meeting, I had three electronic reading centers set up, and all the kids' names typed into my grade-book program on the computer. I had to find some time tomorrow to get back into my classroom. I still had a ton of work to do. At the very least the walls needed to be decorated. I'm not big on emblazoning the classroom in glory and ecstasy rivaling the Sistine Chapel, but I had some pleasantly soothing posters I liked to put up.

At quarter to four, I left. I checked the door twice to make sure it was securely locked.

I followed Georgette's directions to Agnes Davis's house. The message simply said she would have a friend with her who had also been at the meeting.

I drove into the older section of River's Edge off Wolf Road. Agnes lived in a home built in the last century. It was a pleasant Victorian structure—no turrets, but a little filigree decoration over a lintel. A solid, reassuring home, the kind your grandmother owned when you were a kid.

Agnes answered the door and led me into a parlor furnished with enough antiques to fill a collector queen's most vivid wet dream. Agnes and the furniture and the house matched perfectly—both gave off a warm, cozy, safe, secure feeling. Beautiful wooden molding framed all the doors and ran along all the walls on both the floor and ceiling. Heavy wooden furniture. Hardwood floors, highly polished with finely woven area rugs carefully laid near or under various pieces of furniture. A solid rocking chair. A minimum of lace doilies. Portraits of frowning males and females lined the walls. The backgrounds were dark and gloomy, the colors of the clothes on the people all gray fading to black. Sepia-tinted photographs sat atop a mantelpiece. They showed a young couple on their wedding day. Fresh flowers in bright-colored vases on every open surface kept back thoughts of a gloomy Victorian mausoleum.

"Beautiful flowers," I commented.

"Thank you," Agnes replied. "I grow them myself. How is Meg?" I gave her the information I had.

A woman of about Agnes's age sat on a divan. She was Stephanie Quinn. We chatted about the heat while Agnes served tea. The little sandwiches and cakes were delicious. I hadn't eaten anything since breakfast. Agnes smiled encouragingly as I began wolfing down a large quantity of everything.

When I'd finished eating and was sitting back and sipping tea, Agnes began. "We wanted to talk to you. Stephanie has known Meg as long as I, back from before she got married when she first moved to town. We want to help. I was too exhausted last night. I'm not sure anything I told you made sense."

"You were excellent."

Agnes smiled. "I taught first grade in the River's Edge School District for thirty-five years. I remember when you started, Tom. You were such an earnest young man."

To my amazement, I blushed.

"I've been trying to remember more from last night," Agnes said, "and Stephanie knows everyone in the community. She keeps up on everything."

Which I translated to mean, she was a gossip. Excellent. Here were tales that could be told. These were the kind of people who could fill in important background information.

"We know Meg didn't do the murder," Agnes said. "We've been friends for so long. When I talked to the police, I'm afraid I didn't tell them everything. I wasn't sure what to say. I didn't want to get innocent people in trouble, but I wanted someone to know the information I have. It might help Meg. I know you said you'd be helping her."

Stephanie added, "Meg always says the nicest things about you and your friend, the baseball player."

I said, "Meg's a good friend."

"Well," Agnes said. She put down her cup of tea. "That meeting last night was just symptomatic of what's wrong in

River's Edge. People have been so angry in this community since that school board election."

"It all came out in the open at that time," Stephanie said, "but it's been brewing for many, many years."

"What has?" I asked.

"Feuds, petty jealousies, some real dislike. Now it's all turned to hatred." Stephanie was well launched. She wouldn't need much prodding from me. "See, the Quigleys and the Muffins belong to the same Baptist church. They were newcomers back when this town was mostly Episcopalians and Lutherans. People weren't particularly prejudiced, it's just that they were outsiders, a lower class of people. That feeling is gone mostly, but there is still a residue. That's just one example. Those past angers, hatreds, and feuds come out in the open once in a while. Particular events have brought it out more strongly at certain times. Forty years back there was a mayoral race that was very unpleasant. About twenty years ago there was a stink about a prom-queen election. People hardly remember reasons anymore. They do remember discord and anger."

"Half of the time the fights were about silly nonsense," Agnes added.

"But taken very seriously by those involved," Stephanie said. "Then in the last school board election, Belutha, Lydia, and their faction decided to commit themselves to winning at all costs. Those of us who had been around a long time rallied against them. We were happy when the union got so involved."

"You saved all of us," Agnes said.

Stephanie continued, "What you don't know is that there are splits among their faction. Belutha and Lydia don't care for each other that much. Their families used to take vacations together, but they had a falling out. There have been a few public displays of anger among their own kind. Also, we heard there was at least one school administrator who was involved and that Jerome was in the middle of all this. He cared passionately about who won the school board election, and he was furious with the union for endorsing the other candidates. He hated Meg. He was also angry with the way Lydia and Belutha conducted themselves during the school board election. He didn't think they acted with enough class and dignity. He thought there were strategies they should have adopted. Jerome was running for union president to turn everything around. He wanted to ruin the union."

"Are you sure about this?"

"I picked up bits and pieces here and there and put it together," Stephanie said. "I'm sure I'm right. He believed in sneakiness, secrets, and lies behind your back. He'd never confront anyone openly."

Agnes nodded to back her up.

"Is there anybody else you know who could add to what you told me?"

"That's why we didn't want to tell the police. There really isn't one source. You have to know the people involved to come to the correct conclusions."

Which meant they didn't have a direct source. They could be making it all up, or it could be terribly distorted gossip, or it could be valuable information.

Stephanie concluded, "We know the three of them were very angry at each other. I'm sorry we can't be more specific."

"Do either of you know anything about Jerome's family?"

Agnes said, "From watching all the crime shows on television, I know you have to always look to the family first. I don't know them personally."

"Nor I," Stephanie said.

"I can check it out later."

"The important thing is that those people disliked each other so much," Agnes said. "You have to look at each of them very carefully."

I promised I would. I got up to leave and Agnes rose with me.

At the front door she said, "Did you know I was the second president of the union?"

"No," I said.

"Yes, I helped found it. Unfortunately, the first president was completely incompetent. There was a contested election and she lost."

"Anybody I know?"

"It was Beatrix Xury."

"I didn't know that."

"It was long before you were hired. We're talking about ancient history here. I'd been in the district only a couple years at the time. It must have been Beatrix's third or fourth year of teaching. She was one of the ones who led the charge for the union, but she was running it into the ground. A few of us rallied around to save it. I love the union. In a contested election, I beat her. The administration gave me a hard time for a few years about my union activity, but I survived and so did the union."

I thanked her for her information and left.

I certainly hadn't been aware of most of what they had told me. The most disturbing thing was Jerome's plan for the union. I wondered if Kurt had known about Jerome's secret opposition during the school board election. Someone deliberately working against the group was serious stuff. That Beatrix was an early founder of the union and a loser in a tough election was news. No wonder she was bitter about the union and impossible to deal with.

By the time I got home it was nearly five-thirty. I decided to take a nap. Serious napping is an art I excel at. I woke at seven. Scott wasn't home. I called the airport and they said the plane was an hour late. I tidied up the house a little. Scott is a neatnik and I'm a slob, but I like to have all the loose stuff picked up off the floor and all the books in the bookcases and the magazines in neat piles.

After that I got a twenty-four-by-eighteen-inch piece of construction paper from my office. I keep a supply of basic school materials at home. I sat at the kitchen table and began making a chart of everyone's movements the night before. I put all the names I had so far down the long end of the rectangular paper and then the times in fifteen-minute intervals along the top.

At eight-thirty, the buzzer rang. Scott had installed a super-high-tech security system including a gate far down the road that could only be opened by someone pushing a button in the house or with the remote control devices both of us carry on our key rings. The buzzer always rings whether it is opened legitimately or not.

I looked through the camera, as he always insisted I do. I saw a black limousine. The back window rolled down, and I saw Scott give a brief wave.

I left my chart. From the front door I watched him give the driver a tip. By the time he got his suitcase out of the trunk, I had reached the car. Ignoring the driver, who was pulling away, we hugged fiercely in the humid night. The light from the door framed our embrace. I felt his legs and torso slump against mine.

"It's so good to be home," he murmured. I held him until the buzz from the intercom interrupted us. The driver wanted to be let out. I hurried to the control panel in the house. I opened and closed the automatic gate.

Scott put a tape of several early Judy Collins albums on the stereo. He turned off all the lights and lay down on the living room couch. I sat down next to him. He scrunched forward and put his head in my lap. Through the picture window we could see the masses of stars in the early-evening summer sky. Light from a full moon streamed through the windows into the house.

"It's so beautiful," he said. "So restful."

I stroked his chest.

"You hungry?"

"They fed us on the plane." He nuzzled closer. "I don't ever want to move from this spot. I am so exhausted."

"How was this morning's interview?"

"I'm not sure I remember. I think it was one of the nicer ones. I do know I just don't care anymore. I don't want to think. I don't want to lift a finger."

Holding, touching, caressing a six-foot-four baseball player is as sensuous as everybody imagines. I'm the one who gets to touch the stud athlete after the cameras are gone and the crowds have gone home. I know that sounds prideful, but loving him deeply was the foundation on which my actions were based. I know half the gay men and plenty of straight women would be hugely envious, but right then I was more concerned with being able to touch and soothe him. I opened his shirt and caressed the blond down on his chest. He shut his eyes. It was just so comforting to have him home. At that moment, I didn't want him to ever leave again.

Sometime later he muttered, "This is perfect." He

turned so that he was lying on his side, his cheek resting on my abdomen, and his arms now encircling my torso. He hugged me tightly. I returned his pressure. He moved his torso back a little and unbuttoned my shirt. He began caressing my chest. I leaned down and kissed him.

An hour later we lay on the floor staring out at the moonlight and stars. He was twining his fingers through the hair on my chest. "That was even more perfect," he said.

I murmured, "Yes. Did you want to go to bed?"

"I'm not sleepy."

"Me neither."

"An ice cream snack?"

"We have chocolate-chip-cookie dough and extra-chocolate syrup. I made sure there was an adequate supply."

"Saint Tom."

I pulled on my jeans and he donned his white Jockey shorts for our date with the ice cream. We moved my chart to the other half of the kitchen table. I leaned over close to him to set out the ice cream. I love the way he smells— faint hints of his aftershave, sweat, and sex. A mixture of masculine and mellow. We both ate out of separate half-gallon containers.

"What's this?" he asked, pointing with his spoon at my work.

I explained about Meg.

"I'm sorry," he said, "I didn't ask about what was happening with you."

"Helping you through this is more important than school. I like Meg a great deal, but you come first."

"Getting us both through all this publicity is important. You're half of it."

"You're the star."

"Yeah, well, shit happens. How have you done on helping Meg out?" He examined the chart as I talked.

"She gets out on bail tomorrow. I've got to go to court. School starts the next day." I explained what had happened so far. I finished with Trevor's request for a date.

He said, "If this were a story, we could call it 'A Groupie for Tom.' "

"He's pretty in a kid kind of way. I prefer a real man. The big problem is I don't like him."

"Not a solid basis for an affair."

I leaned over and kissed Scott.

"You need bail money for Meg tomorrow?"

"You want to come with me? Todd said we could work it out down there."

"Sure." He pointed at my chart. "You don't have Meg on here."

"Well, of course not. She didn't do it."

"Her movements need to be on here anyway, don't they? And how do you know she didn't do it?"

"I beg your pardon?"

"She's our friend, but look at what's happened with all this gay controversy. We've seen friends and family do nutty stuff. People we've never expected to support us have. Others we thought would be great have turned their backs on us. You don't know the interrelationships between all these people. How do you know she didn't do it?"

"She's a friend. I know her. She wouldn't."

"Did you hear her say she didn't kill Jerome?"

"No." I thought back to my talk with Agnes in the police station. "Agnes didn't say specifically. Maybe, like me, she just assumed she didn't do it."

"I hate to say this. I like Meg too, but what if she did do it?"

"That just sounds so absurd." My mind rebelled against the concept, but now that the seed was planted, I knew I had to check it out.

"I don't think you can leave anybody out unless you are absolutely certain they have an ironclad alibi."

"I'll keep everybody on the list."

"What if it wasn't somebody who was at the meeting?"

"I don't see how we could interview everyone not there. That would be several billion people. I have to start somewhere. I'm going to call Frank Murphy in the morning and see if he can't give me some hints from the police perspective."

"If I can help, let me know." He yawned.

We put the leftover ice cream away and walked arm and arm to bed. We crawled in, but it was quite a while before we were finished and ready for sleep. I dozed off with his arms around me and my head on his chest.

When I awoke, it was still dark. Looking out through the picture window in our bedroom to the new forest, I saw the moon had set. I reached for Scott in our king-sized bed, but he wasn't there.

The bathroom door was open, but there was no light on. I didn't hear or see him. I threw on some jeans.

I found him in the living room. He was sitting in a corner of the couch. The stereo was on low. I could hear the music playing softly. He was listening to a compilation tape of the saddest and most mournful, overwrought, melodramatic country-and-western songs of the past thirty years. He had put it together from hundreds of CDs. He listened to it mostly when he was deeply depressed.

He looked up when he heard me come in. I sat on the arm of the couch next to him. He wore only his briefs.

In the light of the stereo I could see a tear on his cheek. I held his hand. "What's wrong?"

He lifted my hand to his lips and kissed it. "I love you." He rose and walked to the floor-to-ceiling windows. He stood with his feet widespread. He placed his palms flat against the windows and leaned forward. He looked totally studly, but I was worried. I followed him and stood next to him.

"What is it, Scott?"

"When I was a kid and realized I had feelings for guys and not girls, the strongest wish I had was to be normal. To wish I didn't have those feelings. Over and over again I wished for a magic potion to make me straight. I haven't thought about that for a long time, until tonight. I can handle pressure. You know that."

I've seen him pitch some spectacular games of baseball in pressure-cooker situations including no-hitters in the World Series.

I put my hand on his shoulder.

He continued, "I hate all this publicity and pressure. This being emotionally on the edge with half the world discussing my sexuality. I just don't want to take it anymore. I don't want to do any more radio or television shows. I want to stay here with you and hide."

"We can tell them to cancel everything."

"Until the baseball strike is over, and then I'll have to pitch. I want to pitch. If I wasn't gay, I wouldn't have any of this hassle. Is my life, are our lives always going to be like this? I want it to change."

I remembered saying that to the first person I came out

to when I was a teenager. I knew how he felt. "I think our only choice is to be who we are."

"I know what I am and who I am. I'm just tired of wasting so much energy over who we are."

"I understand."

He stopped leaning against the window and put his arm around my waist. He said, "I love you so much. I couldn't get through this without you. I don't know what I'd do if I ever lost you."

I squeezed his shoulder and wrapped my arm around him. "I'm not going anywhere."

For the third time since he'd been home, we made passionate love.

Scott was quiet the next morning. He had nothing scheduled, but he got up and ate breakfast with me.

"You okay?" I asked.

"Yeah, I think so. I needed some sleep in my own bed with you nearby."

"You had me a little worried."

"We've both had more pressure about our private lives than anybody, except maybe the most prominent politicians. I never dreamed of anything like that happening. Last night was a bad moment. Finally being home and at ease let loose all those emotions that running around had kept at bay. Don't worry, I'm not turning into a self-hating gay person, like Trevor."

For some reason, through all the regular early-morning activities I found myself brushing up against him, touching him, wanting to soothe and caress him. He noticed and smiled and took me back to bed for a lengthy and gentle session of pleasure.

I called Todd and checked the exact time of Meg's bail hearing. It would not be until late morning.

Scott decided to stop at his penthouse in the city before we met in court. I drove to the River's Edge police station for a prearranged meeting with Frank Murphy.

Frank's eternally rumpled suit looked rumpled, as rumpled suits are wont to look.

I sat across from his desk. He drank Thunder Bay Clear water.

"Can you tell me anything about what's happening with Meg's case?" I asked.

"You know about the fingerprints?"

"Right."

"It's not my case, so I don't know much more than that. Word is the two of them didn't like each other."

"That part I know."

"I can't give you specific information. Mostly I don't have it, so we don't have to go through that song and dance about what I can tell you. I do know from the talk after everybody got back from the school yesterday that there are a lot of people who do not like a lot of other people in that school and in this town. The fights have been political and personal from races for mayor to infighting in organizations like the PTA. I wouldn't want to be working at the school. Sounds vicious and nasty."

"You remember any names in these fights?"

"Not specifically, although Meg seems to have been in the thick of a lot of it."

"She was always concerned about the community, and she loves to gossip."

"Have you thought of the possibility that Meg might have done it?"

I didn't answer for a few moments, then nodded. Honesty with Frank was important.

"Not a pretty thought," he said.

"Why would Meg kill him?"

"The police aren't working on motive here. They're sticking to hard evidence. Fingerprints on the murder weapon are not a good thing."

"But they could have gotten there during the normal course of her working day. It was a book in the library and she is the librarian."

"But there were no other prints on that encyclopedia."

"There should have been from kids, other teachers, somebody."

"No, this is more a librarian reference book. It's kept behind the desk. No one else has access to it."

"The killer did."

"Yeah. Let me tell you, Tom, the detectives on the case are convinced Meg is the killer. This wouldn't be the first time the disputes in a small community spilled over. River's Edge isn't that unique."

"Any suggestions on who in the community I should start with?"

"A lot of the immediate problem seems to be connected to that school board election. I'm not saying you should investigate this. I do know that if I was looking for more information I'd talk to some of the candidates."

# 8

The first person I ran into at school was Beatrix Xury. I wondered if she kept a periscope in her room so she could watch for me. Or a "Tom Mason Radar Detector."

Her first words were, "Did you call about the air-conditioning?"

I said, "Beatrix, you've been here nearly thirty-five years. What do you know about the fights in the community?"

"Nothing."

"Come on, Beatrix. You must know some of these people. I need some information."

"Well, I don't think I know anything." She trotted away. I wondered if bringing up the murder would be enough to drive her away every time. Only for the briefest moment did I think how convenient it would be for me if there was a murder every day. "A murder a day keeps Beatrix away"—as a saying it had a certain oblique charm.

I found Georgette in the office.

"How's Meg?" she asked.

"I should see her later this morning at the bail hearing. I hope she's okay."

"I do too. She's so wonderful."

"Aren't you going to miss Jerome?"

"We didn't talk much." Georgette leaned closer. "He kind of abused the secretaries. He'd be mean to us for no reason. I know Mavis especially tried to be extra nice to him, but Jerome was real nasty anyway. It started with little things. Like he was always late turning in his paperwork."

"Late grades?"

Georgette rolled her eyes. "Every single time. You know we hate to get teachers in trouble. Sometimes we cover for people, but he was just impossible. He turned nothing in on time. Forms for parking permits, forms for faculty admittance to extracurricular events, just everything. We wound up chasing around after him year after year. Most of that little stuff is due at the beginning of the year, and who has time then or ever to monitor somebody who should know better? When we would remind him about these items, he would be rude and surly. I can tell you this, Tom, but no one else. Jerome was not real popular in this office. Nobody's glad to see him die, but still . . ."

"At this time of the year, I'm surprised you've had time to help out with Meg."

"No matter how crazy it gets, there are certain priorities. She's one of them."

"Any more angry phone calls about me?"

"No, things have started to calm down already. Maybe the murder distracted your detractors. We're working on getting a crisis team in here in case faculty or students need help coping with Jerome's death."

"Do you know who Jerome's friends were on the faculty?"

"A couple people in the math department." She wrote down several names. "The head of the department is in today."

I decided to start with him. Lester Piesman was in his classroom. Half of his walls were decorated. I had to get into my room sometime today to get more done. A calculator bulged from Lester's T-shirt pocket. He wore dark horn-rimmed glasses. His hair was thinning on the top, so he'd combed it over from the sides to try to fill in the gaps. He wasn't fat, but his stomach had started to protrude over his belt. His T-shirt had math equations stenciled on the front and back. It's good to be enthusiastic about what you do. When I entered, he was tacking a poster of Einstein to the front bulletin board.

His greeting was friendly but not effusive. He had a large fan blowing hard. I stood in the draft. The school was too warm already. I tried to picture the OSHA police hauling away custodians and administrators. This thought cheered me up.

Without preamble Lester said, "It is such a shame about Jerome. Is the union going to send flowers? I already arranged for it from among the department members."

"I'll have to check." Another thing to do.

He continued, "He was a good math and calculus teacher. He really knew his subject and he could get kids to really learn."

I almost said, "Really," but thought better of it. I said, "I'm trying to help out Meg. I know she didn't kill Jerome. I want to find out who did."

"In this department, we got along okay. We had a few squabbles, although not as many as some. In the English department, before Jon Pike, you guys had squabbles. With Jon Pike, you have squabbles. It's not too different over here. Nobody was ready to kill over the differences."

The academic departments in high schools fight about a variety of things: their budgets, who in the department got how much money to spend on supplies, or who got to teach which classes—the bright kids, the slow kids, or the specialized, most desirable electives. This last was important. If you had nasty teachers with a rotten reputation teaching the electives, fewer students would sign up for them. The enrollment in your department goes down and teachers lose jobs.

"He ever have fights with anyone in the department?"

Lester thought a minute. "No, not really. We aren't perfect, but we got along okay."

"Did he talk much about running for union president or his campaign?"

"I never did follow that very well. What he told us was that he was afraid this Seth person would get in and ruin everything."

"Like what?"

"You know. Those elementary teachers keep trying to transfer over here. We can't let that kind of thing happen. We could get people in here who aren't qualified to teach higher levels of math. This isn't simple arithmetic."

Seth had mentioned this earlier. Purists in the high school departments wanted only people who had majored in their field to be hired. Elementary teachers tended to have general ed certificates with a minor in or barely enough hours to qualify for teaching in a specialty. This horrified the superspecialized high school teachers who might have fifty or more hours in their major. The superior attitude of the secondary teachers infuriated their elementary colleagues.

"Jerome promised us he'd make sure none of those underqualified elementary teachers would make it into our department. He had some pretty strong support here."

"Did he ever remind you the union has no control over hiring and firing?"

"I guess I knew that, but he seemed so positive."

"How could you believe him? He was so totally wrong."

"You sure?"

"Yes."

"Why would he say it if it wasn't true?"

"He was a lying sack of shit and desperate to be elected."

"Oh."

"He ever make comments about a social agenda?"

"Not to me. He never seemed to care about that kind of thing. He just didn't want the elementary teachers taking over. I don't think he had a lot to criticize about what Kurt's done. I think Kurt's done a great job."

"Do you know if Jerome was involved much in the politics in the community?"

"He never talked about that kind of thing to me. As far as his dealings with the community, everybody has the usual hassles with parents over the years. He had a few more complaints about grades than most since he was such a tough grader. But you've got to have standards or what's the point of grades? His standards were high and I had no quarrel with them."

"He get a lot of complaints?"

"Not really. One or two a year at most."

"No arguments of any kind with coworkers?"

"At lunch it was kind of odd. If he was around, we didn't discuss certain topics."

"Like what?"

"Religion. He's in one of those very strict religions—no cigarettes, no alcohol, no going out to movies. We'd be kind of careful around him. Nobody swore or anything if he was nearby, but he never tried to convert anybody. He left us pretty much alone. I think he did have some fights in the community about his religion. Maybe I heard something about that." Lester thought a moment or two. "Nothing comes to me."

"Did you know his family?"

"I met his wife a few times. She seemed very nice. She was in early this morning to clean out his desk. She was pretty broken up. I helped her with his stuff. She only took a few pictures and a couple of other personal items."

"He have any close friends here at school?"

"Try Deliphinia Schuster. I think she's in."

Deliphinia was in her classroom. All of her bulletin boards were decorated. There were charts on one wall about class rules. More charts listed goals and expectations for each unit. One to be taught each month. Two per quarter. Another huge chart listed dates for the quizzes and final tests to be given on each unit. When I walked in, she was staring out the windows at the stunted trees that surrounded part of the parking lot.

When I entered, she smiled at me. I'd helped her untangle a parent complaint several years ago. She'd been accused of clipping her toenails in class. For one of the few times in her tenure as principal, Edwina had stuck up for her teacher right down the line. Delphinia said it was absurd and it never happened. To my amazement, Edwina had believed her, not argued, and all but told the parent where to stick it.

Deliphinia plucked a tissue from a box and dabbed at her eyes. "It's sad about Jerome," she said.

"You were good friends?"

"Yes. We knew each other at the University of Southern California. I'm from the northern suburbs. When there were no jobs up there, he told me about the opening here. He went out of his way to be nice. I know his wife, Dana. We went to a movie the night of the meeting. She is such a nice, gentle woman. She is totally broken up over this."

"Did you talk to Jerome before the PTA meeting?"

"No. We talked the day before. He didn't really want to go, but he felt like he had to. He wanted to show up Seth." She shook her head. "I told him no one would care, but he didn't listen to me."

"Do you know if he had planned to meet with anybody specific while he was there?"

"No. Why do you ask?"

"I don't think Meg is guilty."

"I only know her a little. She always seemed like a nice person. I can't imagine anyone wanting to hurt Jerome."

"Did he seem like he was anxious or worried about anything lately?"

"No, he was looking forward to school starting."

"Did he have any enemies?"

"No . . . well, he disliked Seth, but I'm not sure they ever met. It was just an election thing."

"Did he have any arguments or fights lately?"

"He and I discussed all kinds of things. When we disagreed with each other, we said so, but those aren't arguments. During the school year, he and I ate lunch together every day. In the summer we talked on the phone at least once a week. Sure, you have to make allowances for friends, but he was a good person. I'd know if there were fights."

"What about in the community? I heard he wasn't happy with the school board election."

"I know you've been a union official for a long time and you were very helpful, but he wanted to change some things. I think change is good once in a while. With Kurt retiring, he thought this was his chance."

"Did he get along with Belutha Muffin and Lydia Marquez?"

"He talked about them once in a while. Weren't they in the same church? He never said mean things about them. Jerome was never mean."

Her tissue caught another tear. She looked around her classroom at her charts and dates and deadlines. "You can be incredibly organized and terribly efficient," she said, "but it doesn't stop a tragedy from happening."

"Being a slob doesn't stop it either."

"No, I guess it doesn't." She blew her nose and almost smiled.

I left. I needed to get moving to make it to the courthouse in Markham where Meg would have her hearing.

When I arrived, Scott and Todd were talking outside the courtroom. All three of us were dressed in dark suits and somber ties. Todd's was flat black. Hard to outdo Todd when it came to depressing clothes.

Todd went over the procedure again, then said, "I think Meg may have enough for the bail. Her house is paid for, and that's what she'll probably use as collateral."

"If she needs anything, we're ready to help."

Todd nodded. "I'll go through everything with her and then I'll talk to her awhile. We'll meet you downstairs later."

When her case was called, Meg was brought in. She hung her head and never looked left or right. The hearing itself took only a few minutes. Meg was given bail of a quarter of a million dollars. A half hour of paperwork later, we finally met in the main hall of the building.

I rushed up to give her a hug. Instead of putting her arms around me, she pulled away.

"What's wrong, Meg?"

"I've been accused of murder."

"I want to talk to you about that. I've been talking to a lot of people."

"Don't."

"Pardon?"

"I don't want you to do anything."

"What's wrong? Did something happen in jail?"

I looked at Todd. He shrugged.

"If you mean was I mistreated, no. Nothing happened. I don't want help, at least not from you."

I was totally confused and hurt.

"I've begun to unearth some important stuff, I think. If you could tell me a few—"

"I'm not going to be able to tell you anything. I want to go home. Please leave me alone."

No one else was there to drive her.

"Scott and I can take you."

"No."

Todd volunteered and she accepted.

I looked from one to the other. Meg had not met my gaze the whole time. She looked completely worn-out and very depressed. She walked on a little way past us. I touched Todd's arm. He held back a moment.

"What's going on?" I asked.

"You know as much as I do. I told you. People get down. You can't help her if she doesn't want to be helped. Leave her alone for a little while. You've been good friends for a long time. Give her some space. This has been the most humiliating and most embarrassing moment of her life. At least I hope it has. She needs time to assimilate all this. She's going to have to have some fighting spirit. In time that will happen. You need to be there then."

We caught up with Meg.

I said, "I'm going to keep digging, Meg. I'll prove you're innocent."

"I don't want you to do anything," she repeated. It was a weak snarl, but a snarl nonetheless. I never expected to hear her speak to me in that tone. "Stay out of my life."

She stalked away. Todd hurried after her.

Scott and I stared after them until they disappeared, then turned to each other.

Scott said, "Something bad must have happened while she was locked up."

"I have never seen her like that. She's never snapped at me. Maybe Todd will have an insight and some information later."

"He can't tell us if she told him something in confidence."

"I know." I shook my head. "I am stunned."

"Or maybe nothing bad happened," Scott said. "Maybe she meant just what she said."

"I can't believe that."

"She sounded awful definite."

"But she's been a friend. I'm not going to abandon her just because she's in trouble."

"She specifically asked you to."

"How can I?"

"You don't want to believe what she said, because if you did, you'd have to accept the fact that a friend you've been very close with for a long time no longer wants you as a friend. That's not easy to take. Especially when she didn't give you any reason why."

"It's because she's worried."

"Tom, maybe she's guilty."

"Is this the way a guilty person would act?"

"I don't know and neither do you."

"Why wouldn't she want help with the investigation?"

"Maybe just not by you."

"Then who's going to help her?" I asked. "She doesn't have any family here. Her ex-husband hasn't talked to her in twenty-five years. I don't even know if he's still alive. She's got a few older cousins down in southern Illinois, I think. That's it."

"Maybe she wants to rely on the police or her lawyer?"

"The cops think she's guilty. Todd will do his best for her, which is a great deal, but is he a criminal lawyer?"

"It's not his specialty. I can't believe what she said to us. Why don't you leave it for now and talk to Todd later?"

I was totally flabbergasted and confused. She'd said some hurtful and harmful things, but I put them down to the terrible strain she'd been under. I could rise above what she'd said because she was a close friend. I began to wonder. Even if you are totally traumatized, do you turn on one of your dearest friends, especially when they are trying to do the biggest favor they could possibly do? Confused, I returned to school. Scott went back to his place to continue canceling engagements and trying to bring some control and order to his life.

I had brought a change of clothes with me so I wouldn't have to work at school in my suit. I changed in the empty locker room, carefully hung my suit on the hanger Scott had stuck in my gym bag, and walked to my room. I found my door still securely locked. Georgette came down as I was opening it.

"How is Meg?" she asked.

"Having a tough time," I replied.

"Poor woman. I'm going to call her later."

"Good idea. She's going to need all the friends she can get."

"Any luck so far?" Georgette asked.

"Nothing substantial. I'm going to keep asking around."

Georgette left. I sat at my desk. As I thought about my last statement, I began sorting out which teachers' editions of textbooks I would need the first week. The kind of idiot work that allows time for rumination. I certainly wanted Meg to be innocent, and I'd done a considerable amount of running around and investing time in proving just that in the last day and a half. And she'd flat out told me to stop. As is so typical, I figured the fault had to be in me. I didn't need a round of self-doubt.

Or putting the blame on Meg. More satisfying and even less productive. Had someone else come and talked to her? Could two nights and a day in jail change someone so quickly? Obviously it had Meg. I know it's hard to accept when someone rejects you, but this was all out of proportion. Or maybe she was guilty.

Then I noticed something was wrong in my room. I stood very still. Something had been moved or changed. A lot of crap was all over every surface. Getting a classroom pulled together requires a lot of unloading boxes of new materials and supplies and unpacking cabinets crammed with paraphernalia. In the process, junk gets scattered hither and yon, but once again, I had the odd feeling that something was wrong. My skin tingled, and my paranoia level skyrocketed.

I walked around the room carefully. As far as I could tell, the papers were where I had left them, and the boxes and trash were undisturbed. The packing material was still in little heaps on the floor, unmolested by a passing custodian.

Then I realized the computer was on. The screen had faded to black, but the little green light that indicated "on" was still lit. I thought I had turned it off. In fact, I was sure I had turned it off. Little niggling doubts surfaced. I guessed I could forget something like that. But I distinctly remembered doing so.

I flipped the switch for the monitor. The screen filled with gibberish. I tried the commands I knew to get to a different screen. Nothing worked. I didn't want to just turn it off. I didn't know what that would do. I knew enough that you aren't supposed to turn off computers without exiting all functions. I'd been warned that if I did so, I could harm the computer or mess up my data or destroy my computer or inadvertently erase all the memory banks in the Pentagon or, as far as I knew, start a thermonuclear war. You can't be too careful or too paranoid in the electronic age.

Like most of us dabbling in the cyber world, first I wondered what I had done wrong. Did I inadvertently press a button that erased the memory of every computer in a thousand miles, or had I ruined mine by doing something stupid? I tried to think rationally. I remembered turning off all the functions yesterday when I saved the class lists I'd finished typing. I found the disk secure in its folder in the top drawer of my desk.

I forced myself to not look over my shoulder as I walked down the hall to the computer lab. The district technology specialist, Rita Fleming, was typing rapidly at a computer. At the end of the last school year she'd been given $100,000 to upgrade all her programs and equipment. She was surrounded by mounds of open boxes, yards of plastic wrapping, and an electronic cornucopia. She looked up, typed a few more seconds, then smiled at me.

"Mr. Television Star."

"Until a two-headed dragon shows up."

"I suspect there aren't many of those in this neck of the woods."

"One would do nicely."

After briefly mentioning her trip to Japan with her husband and two kids for four weeks this past summer, she said, "It's terrible about Jerome and Meg. I can't imagine that Jerome is dead and Meg, of all people, is being accused of his murder."

"Did you know Jerome?"

"I probably would have recognized him on the street. Meg I like. Are you helping her?"

"Yeah. Right now I need assistance with my computer in my classroom."

"What's wrong?"

I explained.

She accompanied me down to my room. She fiddled with all the connections. Then she put her hands on top of the monitor, shut her eyes, and said, "Heal."

I smiled. "Does that work?"

"Not often enough." After a few more minuites of fiddling with it, she said, "I'm turning your buddy here, off. I'll probably have to go into its innards after I do to make sure none of programs or the data have been messed up. You have all the setup disks?"

I showed her my little pile.

"You save anything on this yet?"

"My class lists, but I have a backup disk."

"Smart man."

She flipped the computer off, waited a moment, and then turned it back on. I stood next to her and felt like a fool as she typed and screens scrolled by.

Finally she said, "Here's your problem." She tapped several more keys. A message appeared on the screen.

It was simple and terse: "Fuck you faggot" in large, bold letters.

"Somebody doesn't like you," she said.

"I guess not. How'd it get on there?"

"Let me check."

Again she typed and more data flashed by. It took several minutes before she said, "Somebody got into your hard drive and reprogrammed a lot of it. No matter what you would have tried on the computer, it would have come up with this message. I can eliminate the message for now, but before you can use the computer, I'll have to come back for some internal surgery. If you're lucky, it might be as simple as redoing the start-up."

"How much knowledge of computers would someone have to have to do this? Somebody with a computer degree?"

"Half the bright kids in the school could probably do it."

"That many?"

"Yep, or it could have been one of the teachers. Many of them have taken advanced computer classes."

"Any way to find out who did this?"

"Not from the data."

I shook my head. "This is too much."

"Hell of a thing to find on a screen. I'll be in later to finish fixing it. I've got to get to a meeting. Let me shut everything down before I go." She did so.

I told her about all the other problems and about securely locking the classroom.

"Somebody really doesn't like you. Any kids hate you particularly last year?"

"Not that I can think of."

"Maybe it's got something to do with all your appearances. Lots of homophobia running around these days."

"Somebody would have to risk being seen in the school as they tried to get in here."

"Not if it is somebody who belongs here."

Not a cheery thought. One depressed lover, one messed-up computer with a nasty message, one undone and tampered with classroom, one friend who had turned on me, one murder left unsolved.

She left.

Sitting at my desk brooding accomplished nothing. I could brood while I worked. I pulled the posters off their shelf. Numerous unpleasant thoughts jumbled through my mind as I began taping the backs of the pictures. I started with a forest-glen scene. I wished my forest would look like this someday.

I was most worried about Meg, but now a close second was finding out whoever had been sabotaging my room. Was the minor moving around of small items connected to the message on the screen?

After finishing the fifth poster I decided to move on to attaching some bright lettering to one of the front bulletin boards to emphasize the emergency procedure rules. We used to be told to post these every year. Now they've encased them in plastic and riveted them to the wall. I began rummaging in my cupboard for the letters. I knew I had a box of them somewhere. I was reaching behind some books with my left hand when I dislodged a stack of books deep in the shelf. A small cascade of reference books tumbled out.

I reached to pick them up and stopped. Staring up at me was a *Smith's Comprehensive Encyclopedia* covered with what looked depressingly like dried blood.

# 9

Without touching anything more, I examined the cupboard as best I could. Taking great care and using my hanky to touch the encyclopedia, I put all the books back precisely as I had found them. Then I sat down at my desk and considered.

I thought about calling the cops or my lawyer, probably both. As I'd bumped the books, I wasn't sure if I'd left my fingerprints on the encyclopedia. If I had, would the detectives believe my excuses?

More important, what was the damn thing doing there? Who had put it there? How long had it been there? It was at the opposite end of the room from where the textbooks had been turned around. Was it connected to the murder? How could it be? How could it not be? The cops had the murder weapon. Maybe this was another sick joke by whoever had been sabotaging my room. Or were there two murder weapons? Anything was possible.

So far there'd been one thing in my classroom slightly out of kilter at a time, escalating to the computer message. Was this connected to those relatively minor acts of sabotage? Or maybe the computer, the bloody book, and the sabotage were completely unrelated. I had a brief vision of people scampering up and down the halls of Grover Cleveland, like the Marx Brothers maniacally chuckling as I went slightly goofy.

I slowly walked to the exit, eased myself into the hall, and locked the door as best I could. I worried that someone was hiding in the nearby rooms, ready to pounce or laugh at my concern and confusion or accuse me of murder. I found one of the kids doing community service. I asked the nearest custodian if I could borrow the teen for a few minutes. She said sure.

I stationed the kid at the door to my room. "If anyone tries to get into my room, kill them."

He gave me a kind of mopey look.

"Just kidding. Don't let anyone in. If somebody tries to get in, stop them. Call for help if you have to."

This kid proved that you could mix a nonverbal snarl and a nod at the same time. I love teenagers.

I walked to the learning center. The crime-scene tape was gone. I wanted to find out how many *Smith's Comprehensive Encyclopedia*s we had originally and how many were missing. It was absurd to think this was the same one the cops had. Of course, the book could have been from another library. It could have been carried into school in a teacher's briefcase or a student's backpack or gym bag.

Between two metallic bookends, I found four duplicate volumes. Obviously *Smith's Comprehensive Encyclopedia* was a popular resource. I turned on one of the terminals for the computerized card catalog. It confirmed that the encyclopedias were kept only behind the reference desk as the cops had said. It also told me there were supposed to be two more. I could account for both of them.

I gazed out at the stacks of books. I heard the buzz of the clock on the wall behind the checkout desk. I heard it make a soft click. All was mostly silence and the smell of books.

I walked to the front of the room and began a circuit as I imagined Meg had done. I came to a large drop cloth covering one spot on the carpet.

I lifted it up. I saw a small, dark red stain. They'd probably have to remove only that section of carpet. Nothing leapt out and said, "I'm a clue."

I walked back to my classroom. The teenager said nobody had even been down the hallway. He volunteered to help me anytime. Not a snarl in sight. I supposed it was easier work than anything else he had to do. He sauntered off.

I ascertained that the bloody book was still exactly where I had left it and nothing around it had been disturbed.

I chose to stand at the window and stare out. Random puffs of air tantalized me with the promise of a cooler evening. Mostly I stood, sweated, and thought.

Since Meg was such a great suspect, why try to implicate me? What if it came down to a question of her or me as a suspect? What if Meg had put it there to implicate me? Then why a second book in the library with her prints on it? The murderer put one with Meg's prints on it next to the body and one here? Why? To implicate both of us? Whose prints were on this one?

If it was connected to the murder, why hadn't the killer found a way to let the police know it was here? An anonymous call from a pay phone was all that was needed. Maybe the killer had put it there and changed his or her mind. Then why hadn't the killer come back and gotten it?

It was frightfully easy to break into my room, as was evident. Planting the bloody book could have been done at any moment. Maybe it wasn't the murder weapon at all.

What if *all* the messed-up items in my room were connected with the murder? Why would they be? How could they be? One was a set of odd circumstances with today's message moving beyond the practical-joke, simply annoying level. This book implicated me in a crime.

Could there be two murder weapons? That seemed unlikely. Had I left a print when I was reaching back for the letters? If this was the murder weapon, what did the police have?

The killer bashes Jerome over the head. Then gets another encyclopedia and bangs him over the head again? Why? A whimsical killer? An extremely clever killer? This certainly seemed to eliminate Meg as the murderer. Why leave one book with your fingerprints on it near the body and hide this one? Unless you were interrupted in what you were doing? Or somebody saw Meg do what she did and then planted her purse and a second murder weapon near the body? Which would mean she was trying to implicate me and some guardian spirit or raving loony wanted to implicate her. But then why wouldn't that guardian spirit remove the book from my room?

Even more, what was I going to do about the bloody thing? Any moment hordes of police, tipped off by a crazed killer, could swoop into my room. This thought made me uneasy.

My classroom door swung open.

I looked over at the cupboard. I'd covered any telltale signs carefully. My imagination conjured up a neon arrow pointing to a large black *X* on the spot. My heart beat faster and extra sweat oozed from my pores. Carolyn Blackburn did not stare meaningfully in that direction.

"How was Meg?" she asked.

"Not good." I gave her a brief synopsis, leaving out the hurtful things Meg had said and her request for me to do nothing.

"Is she going to come back to work?" I asked.

"That's the latest controversy. The 'fire Meg immediately' crowd has learned that you can't just dump someone unceremoniously. Due process has to happen. Innocent until proven guilty will prevail in this district if I have anything to do with it."

"If she's found innocent, will you keep her here?"

"I won't recommend she be fired. I can't speak for the board. Lydia is doing her best to cause an uproar."

"Maybe Lydia's the real killer. I hear she and Jerome had some difficulties."

"That's more than I know."

"Do Belutha and Lydia get along?"

"You know it's odd, now that you mention it."

"What?"

"They were on the same side in the election and all the controversies, but I've never noticed them being friendly with each other. You'd think they would be."

I mentioned Lydia confronting me in the hall the day before.

Carolyn nodded. "She's a tough case." She was standing near my desk and eyeing the chart I had started at home and brought to school.

"Do the police have everyone's movements on the night of the killing?" I asked.

"I don't know." She gazed carefully at my handiwork. "You've got everybody on the list."

"Everybody who I know was there."

"Including me."

"Well, yeah."

"If it were me, I'd put every possible name. Saving a friend is important."

I wondered if I was still doing that or saving my own butt.

She made several suggestions of people and times I could fill in, then left.

I decided the smartest thing I could do was call my lawyer. I did the guard-the-door thing again. I hurried to call from the English department office.

Todd wasn't in. I asked the secretary to page him.

"Is this an emergency?" she demanded.

I assured her it was.

Todd called back moments later. "I'm on a recess from court. I've got a chance of winning a million-dollar settlement in the next half hour. This better be important."

Rachel was working in a corner. Several other people were on the other side of the room drinking soda. I put my lips on the receiver and cupped my hands around it. I felt like a cheap gangster in a low-budget 1940s crime movie. I spoke slowly, softly, and distinctly.

"In my classroom there is a bloody encyclopedia hidden behind some books."

"Go to your classroom. Stay there. Let no one in. If someone comes to the door, speak to them in the hall. Do nothing until I arrive."

So I returned to my room and did nothing. That's not quite true. I sweated and I worried. A lot.

I hadn't dared continue working on my room. Who knew what fingerprints I might be erasing or adding? By three-thirty I was bored beyond words. I'd thought of trying to get some work done on my computer. Would the bloody-dictionary depositor have touched those keys? He or she would have if he or she was the same person who was trying to mess with my mind. I brooded about that problem for a while. I dared to look in my desk drawers for something to do. It already had to have a million of my fingerprints on it. In the bottom drawer of my desk, I found a paperback book left by one of my students last year. I'd forgotten the thing. The cover and the first ten pages were missing. It was a ghastly, torrid, teenage-torture opus. I was bored. I read it.

At three fifty-five Kurt swung open my classroom door.

As much to keep him out as eagerness to see him, I hurried to meet him. I used our embrace to steer him closer to the door. "It's cooler in the hall," I said as I ushered him out the door.

"How are you?" I managed to ask with a credible display of interest, considering the circumstances.

"I'm terrific. Doing nothing all summer has a great deal to recommend it."

He looked wonderfully tan and fit. He must have lost at least twenty pounds.

He said, "I heard about Meg. How is she?"

"Awful."

I told him about everything except what was sitting in my classroom.

He shook his head when I told him what Meg had done at the courtroom. "She didn't mean what she said, I'm sure," Kurt said. "You're probably her best friend here. She must have just been in shock."

"I agree."

"You've got some solid information. That Belutha-versus-Lydia stuff has got to lead somewhere."

"I want to talk to them, but I don't know how I'm going to get them to open up."

"I'm not sure either. On the other hand, you could call the police anonymously and say Beatrix killed him."

"Don't tempt me." I gave him a detailed account of Beatrix's ravings.

"I hope I don't run into her," Kurt said. "Listening to that woman is the equivalent of having a dentist clean your teeth with a chain saw. How is Scott after all that touring and publicity?"

"Okay, I think. I'm a little worried." I explained about how depressed Scott was.

"I don't know," Kurt said. "I think that's what's been missing in you guys' relationship. Metaphysical angst about your sexuality. I think you'd be a lot more popular, get on more talk shows. Coming out, going back into the closet, having a revolving door on the closet. It has a ring to it. Popular culture likes their gay people depressed or dying. You guys aren't dying, are you?"

"No."

"Then go with depressed."

"You don't think it's serious?"

"I think he loves you deeply. He knows who he is. He was in pain. Like he said, it was a low moment. He doesn't hate himself. Was he as affectionate as ever?"

"Yeah."

"So, it was an momentary aberration. He's the most celebrated gay figure in America and you're right in there with him. Be happy. Be strong. You'll both be fine."

"I wish I had your confidence. Did you see the propaganda Seth put out about the election?"

Kurt laughed. "I've done a good job. I'm sure he's embarrassed about putting out something that stupid."

I wasn't so sure about that. "Is the election still going to happen?"

"I think so."

"We can't let him win."

"Why not?"

"What if he wrecks everything you've fought to build?"

"I'm not going to have another heart attack for them. Let him fight the battles for a while. Let him see what it's like to bat your head against a wall and have nothing happen."

"I guess. Do you know Belutha and Lydia well enough to talk to? Maybe you could go with me to question them."

"No thanks. I care for Meg, but I don't want to be involved in this. I'm glad I was two thousand miles away."

I felt deflated. I was grasping for any kind of help and here was a good friend bailing out on me. I wasn't about to beg either.

I said, "Didn't you tell me Jerome was in favor of gay rights?"

"I don't remember saying that. I don't know if he was or not."

I knew he'd told me. I wouldn't have misunderstood something like that. I was even more discouraged. At that moment I saw Todd coming down the hall. He was in his funereal best, although when brighter light caught his outfit, I thought his suit might be deep, midnight blue instead of actually black.

Todd and Kurt knew each other slightly. We chatted briefly and then Todd said, "I need to speak to Tom about Meg's case. Will you excuse us?"

Kurt gave a friendly wave and walked off.

Todd and I entered my classroom.

He said, "Tell me exactly everything that you did when

you entered this classroom today." He took a yellow legal pad and a fountain pen out of his briefcase. He took notes while I talked.

When I finished that, he said, "Now, tell me everything you can remember doing in here since the murder."

This was tougher, but I did my best.

At the end I asked, "How much trouble am I in?"

"Did you kill him?"

"No."

"Not as much as if you had plonked him."

"That's not terribly comforting."

"How well do you know this Frank Murphy?"

"We're friends."

"We'll call him. You'll probably have to deal with the other detectives, but starting with him will be better."

Todd stayed in possession of the room. I called Frank. He was at the station. I explained the problem.

All he said was, "I'm on my way."

He arrived no more than a few minutes later. I introduced Todd.

"Called your lawyer first?" Frank asked.

"Wouldn't you?" I replied.

"Where's the thing?"

I pointed.

With the tip of a pencil he moved enough books and materials to ascertain something was there.

"Don't touch anything." He ushered us into the hallway. He pulled out a portable phone and called the station. He talked to the detectives in charge of the case and to the lab technicians.

"This is a mess," Frank said. "I don't enjoy having friends of mine mixed up in murder."

Edwina came down the hall. "Why are you all here?" she asked.

Todd took over the explanation. "We believe we have discovered a significant clue that applies to the recent murder investigation."

Frank said, "The police are gathering information. We'll share whatever we can with school district personnel. We're waiting for the crime-scene technicians to get here."

"Crime scene?" Edwina said. "What crime? Has there been another killing? Why wasn't I notified?"

I said, "Nobody else is dead."

"If the police are to be called, I should be notified." Edwina talked administrative babble and Todd replied in lawyer babble for several minutes.

When they finished, I asked, "Can we get some kind of security guard down here?"

Edwina said, "Security firms have been discussed. I have no idea when a decision will be made about hiring and expenditures. We've had to cut back."

"Can't we at least get one of those community service custodians to be on duty here keeping watch? We'd have a chance of catching whoever did this."

"They're supposed to be working."

"Seems to me they're mostly snarling. What would it hurt to post one of them discreetly down the hall?"

"I suppose I could check into it." She left.

Two more detectives in standard-issue rumpled suits approached us. Maybe if I was lucky, I could get the rumpled-suit concession at the next street fair or opening of the next mall. Business would certainly be steady.

The detectives were Leonard Rosewald and Baxter Dickinson. They were both about five feet ten. Each took off his jacket in the heat, and both wore starched white shirts. They expressed no desire to enter the classroom. Thankfully, they were professionals. Always wait for the crime lab. Even I knew that.

I gave a statement with Todd standing next to me. All my lawyer had said was, "Tell the story exactly about what has happened in your classroom today."

I followed his direction precisely. I said nothing about my outside activities: questioning people and checking the library. I included the parts about the little oddities culminating in the message on the computer.

When the cops started to go over it with me again, Todd said, "Once is enough." They stopped.

Having a lawyer on retainer can sometimes be a very pleasant thing.

The crime lab people arrived. We stayed out in the hall while they went over everything. At one point they wanted my fingerprints. Todd told me it was okay to comply. Their investigation took them several long, boring hours. For the last fifteen minutes, I sat with Todd and Frank in the English office sipping soda. Frank expressed mild interest in my summer activities, but he seemed mostly cool and distant. His answers to my questions about his family were short and uninformative.

Eventually the two detectives came back. Rosewald said, "The only obvious prints on the book are yours."

So, I had touched it before the books fell. Not good. "Nobody else's?" I asked.

"Yours were the only ones."

"Isn't that kind of odd? It's a well-used book. There should be many more."

"There aren't any others."

"Is it Jerome's blood?"

"We don't know yet. We presume it is. Can we go over your story again?"

"No," Todd said. "He gave you his statement. It was clear and it is all he knows."

We all stared at each other for several moments. All three detectives retired to a room down the hall.

I asked, "Can you tell me anything about what Meg said while you took her home?"

"I know you're hurt by what she said, and I wish I could tell you something positive."

"Attorney-client confidentiality?"

"Except for giving me directions, she didn't say a word. You know I don't pry or push. She's been through enough right now. Just wait. Right now we need to worry about you."

"Am I going to be arrested?"

"The first thing I want to know is if that is Jerome's blood or not. That will be the first test."

Georgette brought down a message from Scott. She leaned down and whispered. "I stayed late when I saw the police arrive. Are you all right?"

"I hope so," I murmured back.

"I've got to go home."

"It's okay."

She patted my arm encouragingly and left.

I called Scott and told him what was happening.

"Are you in danger?" he asked.

"I don't know."

"You didn't tell me about all that strange stuff in your classroom."

"With you being back and the murder, it didn't really seem important until today. It was just pranks before, or possibly forgetfulness. The computer message and the bloody book are real and significant and something that has to be taken care of."

"Do you want me to come down there?"

"I'll let you know."

"I'm glad Todd's there."

"Me too."

Half an hour later Frank, the other two detectives, and I sat in the long-since-deserted English office. It had been impossible to disguise the presence of the cops in the school. No doubt word was winging through River's Edge of this latest twist in the murder case. I was not happy that I was in the middle of it.

Dickinson broke the news. "It was Jerome Blenkinsop's blood."

The cops all looked at me. I gazed at Todd. A cold shudder ran up my spine.

"You want to tell us something?" Baxter said.

"He's given his statement," Todd said.

I was disappointed that Frank just sat there. I'd hoped for a little more backing. My expectations of friends' behavior were not coming true today.

"Where were you the night of the murder?" Baxter asked.

Todd nodded slightly.

"I was at home reading."

"You have any proof for that?"

"I got a call from my lover about ten o'clock."

"We're you on the phone all night?"

Todd said, "I'm sure the phone records will give you the exact times. We'll provide those if you wish."

I didn't really wish, but I was not about to contradict my lawyer.

Carolyn Blackburn walked in. "Excuse me for interrupting. I had left for the day and gone directly out to do some shopping. I came as soon as I checked my phone messages."

The police gave her the scantiest of details about what had been found.

Carolyn said, "This makes the murder investigation more complicated, doesn't it?"

The detectives agreed.

"Now what happens?" Carolyn asked.

Frank suggested he and the two other detectives meet in the hall for a conference.

After they left the room, Carolyn took a seat. "Doesn't this just beat all?"

"Yeah," I muttered. I thought about snarling, but why take my frustration out on her? I gave her more details than the cops had.

"I had three calls from board members on my answering machine. Lydia's was the nastiest. She said she was on her way to the school. I didn't see her, but since I'd been forewarned, I didn't come through the central office."

"I'd like to talk to her," I said. "Just her and me. She knew Jerome better than anybody. I suspect Jerome was holding out on his people here about the election. I believe Lydia would have information."

"Do you think she'll talk to you?" Carolyn said.

"I have questions to ask that I don't think the police are going to ask. If I'm free to talk to people, I want to." I turned to Todd. "Are they going to arrest me?"

"I doubt it. The presence of only your fingerprints and the absence of any others makes it more difficult for them."

"Maybe they think I tried to wipe it clean and simply missed some."

"Plus they'd have to prove some nefarious connection

with you and Jerome. They can't simply arrest all those people who don't have an alibi for that night."

Frank came back into the room. He looked at me. "You're free to go. If I was a tough cop in a movie, I'd snarl something about you not leaving town."

Everybody loves a snarl.

"What do you think?" I asked.

Frank shook his head. "This is a delicate business."

Carolyn interrupted, "I don't want to be present for any kind of legal discussion or anything remotely like it. Can I speak with the detectives who were here? I want to know if we can have our school back."

"Yeah," Frank said.

She left.

"I'm not investigating," Frank said, "but I am a cop. I can be a little more open here for old times' sake. Obviously we have lots of new questions, which is in your favor and maybe even Meg's."

"I've asked myself a million of them."

"The key from our point of view is that if this is the murder weapon, then what have we got in the evidence lockup?"

"Is it still there?"

"Yes. It's been checked. It's the unanswered questions that make the case difficult and at the moment impossible to arrest you."

"Will they free Meg?"

"I don't know. We need to figure out a number of things. Like, if you and Meg were coconspirators, why leave fingerprints on one weapon, but not the other? Or why not wipe both clean? Or did you simply miss a spot? If you wiped your fingerprints off, why is the blood still there? Why hide one book but not the other? Better yet, why put this one in your room? Storage? Why is it still there? Forgetfulness? Why wait and call the police on yourself several days later? I suggested some of these things to them."

"Thanks." I felt better that he was working for me a little.

"Don't thank me. I'm being a good cop. I don't pretend to understand this. I don't think you killed anybody, Tom, but don't let your friendship with Meg blind you. She is a good suspect, but this case has certainly turned bizarre."

"But I haven't done anything."

"What have you uncovered? I can tell the other detectives after you tell me."

The question chilled me. Right then I wasn't prepared to trust too many old friends. This had been too much a cop question, a possible trick question, a cop offer. The kind the dumbest suspects fall for on *NYPD Blue.* I didn't like it that he asked. It was almost like a betrayal. He became more cop than friend at that moment.

"Frank, I think I need to discuss the whole situation with Todd before I say anything."

"I just went to bat for your butt."

I wasn't prepared to explain to him how I really felt. Todd spoke up. "Detective, we are fully cooperating. Tom and I need to talk." He said no more, but the conversation with Frank was obviously at an end. He left.

"Now what?" I asked.

"I go home after having earned another chunk of the retainer you and Scott pay me."

"What can I tell Frank?"

"You haven't interfered in a police investigation. You've been cooperative, but you don't need to talk to them. I wouldn't trust Frank very much."

"He's a friend, or I thought he was."

"You seem to be coming up short in the friend category this afternoon."

I thought of Kurt. "People don't want to be connected with murder."

"Frank's a cop. If you find out anything, call me. I strongly suggest a great deal of discretion if you talk to people. I suggest even more strongly you let the police handle the case."

"I didn't kill anybody. I don't think Meg did. I need to find the killer before I get accused."

"Then realize you will have to talk to the police if you take an active role. I don't think they can make a case against you, but let's err on the side of safety."

I couldn't remember how many times Todd had told me this last. I like a nice conservative, cautious lawyer.

I entered the corridor. All the cops were gone. I stopped in my room and picked up my suit, gym bag, and briefcase. The room was not a shambles. As far as I could tell, the police had removed only the one book.

I was depressed. Frank, a cold and distant cop. Kurt, backing off from helping. Meg, openly hostile.

I had work to do to keep myself from becoming a suspect of some kind, or even thought of as an accomplice.

Carolyn poked her head in my room, then entered. "Lydia Marquez is in the school office. She said she wants to talk to you."

"About what?"

"I'm not sure. I presume it has something to do with the murder. She wouldn't tell me. I'm only the superintendent."

"I'll bring my lawyer with me."

"That's up to you," Carolyn said. "I'm going to go home. There are several park district functions going on in the

144

building so you can just leave by any exit. The custodians will be cleaning until late."

Todd and I walked down the corridor together. He still wore his coat and tie. He never seemed to sweat. Maybe he was secretly dead and simply hadn't told the rest of us. I explained about Lydia.

"Talk to her if you want. Why don't I wait out in the hall just in case you want me? Give her a chance. See what she has to say."

# 10

Lydia was in her tent jeans, but had added a tent blouse over her mounds of flesh.

We sat in Edwina's office. Lydia rested her bulk in the comfy leather chair behind the desk.

Lydia said, "There's all kinds of rumors running through town."

I nodded.

"Will you tell me what happened?" she asked.

"If you wanted information, why didn't you just ask Carolyn?"

"Carolyn is an employee like you. You're the one who is directly involved."

"Is this a hostile conversation or any kind of investigation? My lawyer is right outside."

"No, no. That's not necessary."

"Mrs. Marquez, I don't mean to be rude, but what is this all about?"

"I wanted to talk to you. We've been on opposite sides, and we've never really spoken with each other."

"All you had to do is come talk to me. The only remote contact we've had is because of the race for school board. I just worked with the union in the election campaign."

"Against me and my friends."

"Yes."

"That's your right, but I was dissatisfied with our chat in the hall. We may never be friends, but I'd like to reach a point of benign neutrality. Besides, you're famous. I don't know anybody else who's been on *Oprah.*"

She had chosen this moment to be a star chaser/ groupie? I didn't think so.

"Have you talked to the school board's lawyer?" I asked. "Does she know you're talking to me?"

"Why do I need to consult with the board's lawyer to talk to someone?"

I would have if I were a board member, but she hadn't asked for my advice. "Mrs. Marquez, what did you want to talk to me about?"

"I'm concerned about the district."

"Aren't we all?"

"I'm in a position of grave responsibility. I think we could work together to help resolve this situation. I understand you've been questioning people about what happened."

"Yes."

She leaned forward in her chair. "I'd be willing to trade information."

"I won't make any unconditional promises."

"May I be honest with you?"

What was I going to say? No, lie to me?

"I'm frozen out by most of the other board members. My agenda for change in the schools is not going to happen as long as I always get voted against six to one. I am a practical woman. I'd like to move beyond that."

I wondered what that meant and what it had to do with me.

"I know you think I'm evil incarnate."

I couldn't argue with that.

She continued, "I'd like to have at least a working relationship with you. I think you still have a lot of say in the union. And this mess with Jerome and Meg Swarthmore has me upset."

"How so?" I was surprised to hear my own question.

She drummed her fingers on the desk for several moments. Finally, she said, "I wish things were different. I used to be certain of everything. At one time I was very close to Jerome. His death has upset me."

"You were close?"

"When he first started teaching in the district, he came to my church, but there were feuds among various factions. He left and joined another congregation. Jerome was always kind to me. He reached out to me in some difficult times early in my marriage. I was sorry when his faction split from ours."

"You couldn't stay friends outside of church?"

"Either you believe or you don't. Those were the options at that time. I've learned some since then. Too often we've been too rigid. I still believe, but I think our tactics have to be professional and sensible. Always screaming at the top of our lungs is not the way to get people elected. My confrontation with you in the hall was inexcusable. I apologize."

"I appreciate that, but I don't understand. If you want to change tactics, how come you caused trouble at the PTA meeting?"

"You weren't there. If you had been, you would have seen two factions. Belutha going out of control almost lost us the election. We should have won that election by at least twenty votes. I'd counted carefully. I or my friends knew who was there and who we could count on. Now with Jerome's death, I'm worried."

"About what?"

"Belutha might have had something to with his murder."

I sat there stunned for several moments. It wasn't that I believed Belutha was inherently innocent. I said, "You're turning in your friend?"

"I don't know what to think. She's been more of an ally I had to put up with than a friend. My faction of the church is not as radical, has more class, than Belutha's. She's made some wild threats. She's not a help to us as a raving loony or as a killer."

"And the attendant bad publicity?"

She had the grace to smile and nod. "Yes."

"But you all three agreed on the same agenda."

"Usually. I was part of the meeting that encouraged Jerome to run for union president."

"But I heard he was in favor of equal rights for gay people."

"Never. He knew about you and your activity in the union. He simply never said anything either way. It was sneaky, but no one ever asked him directly."

"That's kind of mean."

"He loved being secretive, and he was determined to win. I was willing to help him."

"Was he really going to change things if he got elected?"

"Everything he could. He was determined to reverse all the liberal concessions the union had won in the last few years. The union leadership is far more liberal than its members. He was going to speak out for the majority of teachers."

"You're wrong about that, you know. I realize that is conventional wisdom among some politicians, but membership is not clamoring for elected officials to take away their rights."

"We'll see, but I didn't come here to discuss politics."

"No?"

"Belutha was out of control. Every time we met, Jerome and Belutha fought."

"What did they fight about?"

"Almost anything. For example, Belutha wanted Jerome to put out position papers like that Seth was doing. Seth was a true believer, but in his little causes, not in ours."

"He wasn't in your faction?"

"No, he isn't in our churches. I don't know him at all."

"He had no hidden agenda?"

"Not that I'm aware of. Belutha was out of control. She made threats. She wanted to picket, boycott, go to every meeting and disrupt the proceedings. She had to be slapped down more than a few times by others in several public forums. Jerome was one of the ones who didn't like the way Belutha handled herself."

"But Jerome was out of control at the PTA meeting."

"Remember, Belutha had to be led out. Jerome took Meg aside. I must say your friend was not a picture of calm reserve."

"I don't get that last statement. You people sit back and say the most dreadful things, make the most outlandish accusations, and then you try to claim the morally superior high ground if somebody dares to disagree with you."

"That may be, but I thought we'd agreed to help each other here?"

"Why don't you tell the police what you know?"

"Because then I'm involved. I'd have to give statements to them. If I get drawn in as a school board member, it might look bad for the district."

And for yourself, I thought. I said, "I could just tell the police what you told me."

"But we are the only ones here for this conversation. Deniability is a concept that works for me."

"There's got to be a reason you're telling me this. You didn't develop a sudden urge to be friends with Meg or me."

"No. To put it simply, by helping you, I may be able to help myself. If it turns out Belutha is somehow involved, then my life is easier. I don't have to deal with her."

"I'm sure she'd love to hear that. How do you know I won't simply run over to her house and blurt out what you told me?"

"I know you want to free your friend. You'll follow the truth wherever it will lead you. I know that you're at least on the periphery of the investigation. If Belutha isn't guilty, I have lost nothing. If she is, I have gained a great deal."

If I hadn't talked to Agnes and Stephanie earlier, I wouldn't have believed any of this. Even with that knowledge, I wasn't close to buying her whole story, but she was right. If this was information that took suspicion away from Meg and me, great.

Of course, she could also be trying to divert attention away from herself. A distinct possibility.

She said, "I've given you some information, will you in turn share with me?"

I wasn't about to give her anything incriminating. I gave her a scanty outline of the presence of the bloody book.

She said, "So the police have two books with different fingerprints. What does that mean?"

"I don't know."

"I guess I was more thinking out loud." Maybe I was wrong, but I thought there was a sudden gleam in her eye. She'd just thought of something or whatever I'd said had started a train of reasoning she wasn't about to divulge. Or her contact lens had caught the light just right. Who knew?

She nodded several times, seemed satisfied with what I'd said, then she left.

I called Scott and told him I would be home in about an hour and would give him the whole story when I arrived. I looked up Belutha's address on the district master list in the office. Todd walked me out to my car and I filled him in on Lydia's revelations.

"What are you going to do?" he asked.

"I'm not going to the cops, that's useless. It's thirdhand hearsay or something."

"It's not hard evidence."

"That too. I'm going to Belutha's and I'm going to tattle."

He smiled. "You're going to destroy your budding friendship with Lydia."

"She took a chance. She lost. I'll call you if necessary. If there are any developments with Meg, let me know."

I unlocked my black pickup truck. With its oversized wheels, shining black metallic exterior, and black leather interior, I call it the butch mobile. Wishful thinking.

When I turned the motor on, the radio blared enough to hurt my eardrums. Someone had turned the volume to full blast.

I snapped it off. I put the window down and listened to the neighborhood noise. I heard the roar of a motorcycle. When that faded, I listened to kids calling to each other. Children on bikes were riding around on the tennis courts. In the near distance I saw the arc lights around the community baseball field.

For ages Scott had been after me to get an alarm system installed in the truck. I had informed him that it was silly. I'd been told people could get around an alarm system almost as easily as breaking into the car. Scott had informed me that I'd been told wrong. I hadn't listened to him and now I wished I had.

This had to be more harassment. By whom? And what for? Wasn't there enough already? Unless this was not done by the murderer. Or done before all of today's other incidents or without the knowledge of them.

Sitting aimlessly in the parking lot wasn't going to help. There was nothing I could do at that moment about whoever was harassing me, so I drove to Belutha's.

She lived three blocks from Agnes. Her old Victorian home had one turret and a bay window, but was not overly endowed with gingerbread. Lights were on in the ground floor. Through a front window, I saw a large-screen television. On it a fat-faced preacher with a self-satisfied smile waved his arms.

I knocked at the door. A child of about five answered. I asked to speak to Ms. Muffin.

"Mom!" the kid yelled, and disappeared.

I'd never met Belutha. A moment later a moose of a woman appeared behind the screen. Belutha Muffin had the weight but not the height to be a lineman for a professional football team. She filled the doorway in a pale pink muumuu. Using the same comparison, Lydia might have the heft for a linebacker on a college team.

I introduced myself.

"I know who you are."

"I'd like to talk to you."

"Coming here to plead for your job will do you no good."

"I beg your pardon."

"That isn't why you're here?"

Whatever lurid scenarios had gone through her mind, I couldn't be sure. Dramatic confessions on my part? Repentance?

"No, I have some information that I think might be useful to you. May I come in?"

She looked uncertain, but I'd showed up unexpectedly and caught her off guard. She hadn't had a chance to check her Bible and find the correct behavior for what to do when the faggot shows up on your doorstep.

"What information?"

"Lydia Marquez came to talk to me. She tried to implicate you in the murder of Jerome Blenkinsop." I figured I'd start out with the big bomb and work down.

"I don't believe you. Lydia wouldn't and didn't."

"Would you like me to go to the police with what she said instead of talking to you?"

"If Lydia knows something, why didn't she go to the police?"

The same question I'd asked. "Right now it's at the gossip stage, not the hard-evidence stage. Do you think she should be going around telling people nasty stuff about you?"

"What did she say?"

Gossip. About yourself. Good or bad, who could resist? I was directed into the front room. What little I saw of the house was neat and clean. A "God Bless Our Home" sampler and a picture of the Nativity were the only wall decorations. The room I was in had plastic covers on the couch and chairs.

"The children are still little. We don't want them to spill on the good furniture."

She was apologizing for her housekeeping. Something I never did.

The couch cushions squished as I sat down on them.

She asked, "What did Lydia say?"

"She said you and Jerome had fights. That you were out of control. If you were implicated in Jerome's murder, it would remove a thorn from her side and that of your organization. She also said that you had no class and that she didn't like your tactics."

Belutha's face was very, very red before I was even halfway through with this recitation.

"She didn't."

"I suppose she could deny saying those things. She and I were the only two in the room."

She gave me a look of distaste. "You're making this up."

"Carolyn Blackburn saw me go into the office with her. Lydia told me that Jerome had promised to go after all the liberal rules the union had won in the last few contracts."

"She told you!"

"That was the plan?"

"Yes. She did tell you. She did talk to you. How dare she speak to you?"

"I think she doesn't like you."

"Well, I always tried to like her. I suppose I can handle being enemies. She'll be sorry."

Great. I cared if it cleared me or Meg of any suspicion.

"She said the fights were pretty serious."

"Lydia doesn't know what she's talking about. I met with Jerome secretly. He was on my side. People are afraid of Lydia. She's got a sharp tongue and a lot of friends. If I wasn't a Christian woman, I'd have said some hateful things about her."

More and better. "When did you meet with Jerome?"

"Just before the PTA meeting. It was mostly about religious and family things. He was going to come back to my church. He was tired of the backbiting ways at his new place. I offered to help him get into some of the committees in the church."

"That doesn't sound murderous."

"Let me tell you a thing or two. We worked so hard in the last election. We lost those three school board offices by less than a total of two hundred votes. If we could have done just a bit more, we could have taken control. Lydia kept pooh-poohing my ideas. Everything I said was wrong. She thought whatever she said was wisdom straight out of the Bible."

"It wasn't?"

"Not hardly. She kept trying to squeeze my friends out of things. She wanted to take over the school board and be its president."

"Didn't you?"

"The plan was for all of us to get elected. After we won, there was plenty of time to decide who got what."

"But only she won."

"And I won the PTA election. We're making progress. After the school board election, we weren't discouraged. We still had our causes to fight for. We went ahead with the fight for the presidency of the PTA. This special union election gave us another chance. There's a lot of anger in the community about the teachers' union. Those settlements in the last few years have been outrageous. There are some teachers in this district making more than fifty thousand dollars a year."

I thought of numerous responses to that balderdash, but I wanted to get her back on track.

"What happened at the PTA meeting?"

"Your friend Meg—yes, I know she's your friend—did what she's always done to me. She tried to shut me out. She made fun of me and my beliefs. I'm afraid I got out of control. I was so glad that Jerome told her what for."

"Were you there or did you talk to Jerome after he spoke with Meg?"

"I spoke briefly with him afterward. He was very kind and helpful. A true friend. He couldn't talk to me long though. He said he had to meet with more people."

"Did you tell the police this?"

"Yes."

"Did you know who?"

"No. If he'd have told me, we'd know the killer."

"Where did you go when you left the meeting?"

"I went to the teachers' lounge to lie down. I turned off the lights."

"Did you see anything else?"

"I saw that Beatrix Xury still trying to buttonhole people."

Beatrix had told me she went shopping.

Belutha continued, "Is that woman insane? Does she do anything else besides find fault?"

"You noticed."

"While I was running for school board, she would call me and complain and ask if I got elected, would I fix this, that, or the other thing. She was constantly harping. She wanted a change in the school board so we could take care of her personal needs. I couldn't afford to alienate her. She's got a big mouth around town. She supported us."

Traitor Beatrix. At the endorsement meeting no one, including Beatrix, had spoken against any of the union's choices. The vote on whom to endorse was unanimous. I remember Beatrix sitting near me with a fatuous smile on her face.

A child came in wearing pajamas and kissed Belutha good-night. She gave her a hug and a kiss and promised to be up in a minute to tuck her in. I could barely hear the television in this mostly quiet house. Thankfully they had air-conditioned it.

Belutha said, "I saw Beatrix talking to one of those new teachers. A blond, young man, Trevor something. They seemed to be arguing. I couldn't hear what it was about. I didn't tell the police about that. Should I have? As far as I could tell, it had nothing to do with Jerome."

"It probably wasn't important," is what I said, but I wasn't so sure about that.

I'd have to talk to our Beatrix and our Trevor, if that's who it was. The picture of Beatrix as a lying sack of shit appealed to me. Trevor as a total asshole worked for me as well. Of course, if he was arguing with Beatrix, he couldn't be all bad.

I asked, "What did you do?"

"When I felt better, I got up. I was still a little weak. That outburst took a physical and emotional toll on me. I'm on several different medicines from my doctor."

"Did you see anything as you left?"

"I didn't even vote. I left by one of the side doors. I passed Meg on her way down the hall."

"When was this?"

"I said, on my way out. I ignored her. She wasn't on the way to the library. I saw Jerome after that. He was coming back from the wing with the math department offices. He was alive when I left."

Meg had taken a journey outside the room that I hadn't

known about. And what was Jerome doing down in the math offices? Simply stopping in his classroom, or picking up something in the office he forgot, or trysting with a murderer?

"You didn't see Jerome and Meg together?"

"No, they were going in opposite directions."

It bothered me that Meg hadn't added this to what she had told Agnes. Or had Agnes simply forgotten it or left it out deliberately? Or did Meg have something to cover up? I wanted to speak with her. Before the murder, we'd have been comparing notes and making cracks about all the people involved. Now, I'd be happy to comfort her and help her out. I needed a face-to-face meeting with her.

Belutha continued, "I talked with Jerome for another second or two. He'd been to his mailbox and found a note from that Seth person. Jerome was really angry that Seth had put out such a thing."

"I don't remember Jerome's name being mentioned."

"It wasn't. He was afraid it was going to make Seth successful. That people would believe and trust Seth and not Jerome. He wanted to write something against it or something more harsh. He wanted me to begin planning to have another meeting to write it up."

"He didn't write his own propaganda?"

"Oh my, no. We would get together to decide strategy. I shouldn't tell you any more about that."

"You've been helpful." I got up to leave. She showed me out with some graciousness. She added at the end, "I'm going to be on the phone about Lydia tonight. She can't say those kinds of things."

Instead of turning on the air-conditioning in the truck, I left the windows open. A mild sheen of sweat formed on me as

I hurried through the Midwestern humidity. I smelled rain on the wind. I hoped it would make it cooler.

At home I found Scott curled in his favorite armchair. He was watching The Weather Channel on cable television. If he's depressed, he can sit there for hours enthralled by the charts, graphs, and occasional inadvertent hilarity of live television.

"Sorry I'm late."

"There's cold pizza. You want me to microwave it for you? I made a salad or you could nuke some vegetables."

He ate a salad while I had a late dinner. "You okay?" I asked.

I watched him carefully. He was wearing white gym socks and his oldest high school gym shorts. He'd sewn them and patched them numerous times. He wore his working-on-the-car T-shirt. It never came completely clean in the wash anymore. It had interesting patterns of old stains. It also clung tightly to the muscles on his upper arms and showed his flat stomach to great advantage.

"I'm feeling a little better," he said. "I spent most of the day canceling engagements. Biff is not happy with me."

His agent had some long, boring preppy name; Scott just referred to him as Biff.

"Are you happy with you?" I asked.

"Yeah, I guess. As I erased each thing from my calendar, I felt better. I'm keeping only those engagements where I agreed to do a charity appearance. Most of those are AIDS-related anyway."

A huge number of Scott's promotional appearances in the past few months had been for helping other gay people, gay health groups, gay hospices. If it was gay and they needed help, they called Scott.

He continued, "I cut back on some of those too. I want

time to myself. I need to enjoy the first September I've had off since fourth grade."

"I'm worried about you. I'm also having a little cognitive dissonance. We've been fucking like bunnies since you've been back, but you're upset about being gay?"

"Is that cognitive dissonance stuff catching?" He felt my forehead. "You don't have a fever and you don't look cognitive or dissonant."

"I think you're better."

"I'm still a little down, but I'm pulling it together. My comment came from a mixture of depression and being overtired and a wish that everything could be easier and simpler. I know who I am and I'm happy about it. I'm as normal as I want to be."

I mentioned Kurt's comment about being an unhappy gay person. Scott laughed. "People are more used to dying and depressed gay people from all that shit on television. They're going to be disappointed if they do a film on my life."

"Good."

He asked me about the investigation and I filled him in. I finished, "I'm worried about the union election."

"You get wrapped up in things. Whose side is winning and losing. I've seen you on election nights flipping between every network and cable television station. You are obsessed with this stuff. Are you sure that's good?"

"Isn't it important who wins the union election in my school?"

"Why would it be? How is it going to hurt you if Seth wins?"

"You're the man whose union is making huge headlines about its strike. It makes a difference if there's a moronic fool running things. I think it's important to prevent that.

People invest a lot of emotion in what directly affects their lives. Look at the passion that was involved in the simple PTA election that started all of this. According to what I've learned, a lot of that began many years ago."

He nodded. "You're right. The guys on the team get nuts about the union."

"Nobody stands out as a major suspect yet," I said.

"That Beorn guy, the part-time teacher, strikes me as dangerous. It's always good to have a militia member hanging around the woodwork as a murder suspect."

"Beorn strikes me as mildly nuts, but he doesn't rate too highly as a killer."

"Lydia?"

"Lydia or Belutha work equally well for me, but I don't see major motivation for murder there."

"How about Beatrix?"

"If I could pin the murder on her, I would be delighted."

"Or Meg."

"Possible, but not probable."

"Maybe you need to look deeper into motivation."

"I need to look deeper into everything."

Snuggled together on the living room couch, we watched our tape of the movie *Beautiful Thing*, something that often helps cheer him up. At one in the morning, it began to rain lightly.

When we got to bed, he pulled me close and rested his head on my chest. He rearranged my chest hair with his chin so it wouldn't tickle his nose. I put my arms around him and he sighed contentedly. I stroked his back and his shoulders gently and easily. I was still worn-out from lack of sleep. I was not looking forward to being up in a few hours to go to school.

I'd thought he'd fallen asleep when he murmured, "I love you, Tommy."

Most everybody just calls me Tom. My mother, when she was irritated with me when I was a kid, would call me Thomas—still does. I don't usually like being called Tommy, but when Scott does it with the deep thrum in his voice with that latent Southern drawl behind it, I just melt. We don't call each other pet names often, but that's his for me in his most emotional and tender moments.

I said, "I love you."

I felt his body relax and knew shortly after that he had truly fallen asleep. He seldom nods off all nestled around me, and I usually find it difficult to fall asleep that way as well, but I didn't care that night. I held and caressed the man I love for a long time. It was quite a while before I dozed off.

I woke around six. Scott was still asleep. I noted the tousled hair, the rise and fall of his chest, the occasional murmur or twitch. I still love watching him sleep.

Finally, I got up and looked outside. A light rain switching to mist continued to fall.

I decided to get in a morning workout. Tomorrow was Friday and we would have students all day. Today was a teachers' institute at the new school. The people I wanted to talk to would all be present. I thought of calling Meg. I decided to wait and see if Georgette had talked to her. Maybe Georgette would have an insight I had missed.

I'd been clanking with the weights for about fifteen minutes when Scott joined me. In silence he did his stretching exercises. We wore old sweat clothes shrunken from many washings to where they clung to various muscle groups on our bodies. We spotted each other as we lifted and groaned. About halfway through the workout his crotch brushed against my knee as I was doing a leg lift. I stopped and he moved closer. He brushed the sweat from his eyes. Sweaty sex with that man is just about the best.

A few intense and fierce minutes passed.

I was in the shower when he came into the bathroom. I thought he was going to shave. He pulled the door slightly open.

"You were talking about a Belutha Muffin last night?"

I stopped shampooing my hair. "Yeah. I talked with her at her house last night. She's one of the pains in the asses of the opposition."

"Not anymore she's not. She's dead."

# 11

He'd been listening to an all-news radio station. We couldn't find a report on any other station or a repeat of what he'd heard. I called several friends including Kurt, but they had heard nothing. Everyone was in a rush to get to school for the first institute day. I hurried myself. At the door I kissed Scott and told him I loved him. He pulled me close and grasped my shoulder with one hand and my butt with the other. He squeezed them both.

It poured rain for the entire forty-five minutes it took to drive to work. By the time I stepped onto the pavement in the parking lot, a fresh breeze was blowing and the sky to the north was clearing. Cool after the rain. It was heavenly.

The parking lot of the Benjamin Harrison High School was crowded with the cars of teachers from all over the district. I saw emergency vehicles clustered around a distant door. They were parked on the newly sodded back lawn.

Inside, the school glistened and gleamed. The tile shone. The walls were that massive cinder block so many schools are built of now. The yet-to-be-blemished walls were painted a pale yellow. The glass in the windows sparkled. The air-conditioning puffed merrily away.

I spotted Kurt. He was surrounded by a group of teachers. I joined them. The number one topic of discussion was Belutha.

Numerous voices shared theories and wild rumors.

"I heard she committed suicide."

"No way. I heard she had her throat slit in one of the johns."

"I saw the emergency vehicles out back," I said. "It happened here?"

"Yes," three people said.

"Where have you been?" Kurt asked.

"I just got here. Who has real information?"

One of the group offered, "I heard she had a doughnut stuffed in her mouth."

"Is that significant?" I asked.

"It's what I heard."

"A custodian found the body this morning."

"She'd begun to decompose."

"The custodian or Belutha?" I asked.

"Probably both," Kurt said.

"Well, that's what I was told."

"She wouldn't begin to decompose so soon," another one commented.

Kurt took me aside. "Beatrix is pissed at you."

"About what now?"

"Just about everything, I believe. I'm supposed to holler at you and get you in trouble." He laughed. "I gave her a big hug, and we're best friends."

"Fat chance."

Carolyn Blackburn swept by with the president of the school board and the two detectives Baxter Dickinson and

Leonard Rosewald. The school board president was talking rapidly.

I knew who I had to find. Georgette. On the first institute day the secretaries usually had folders and name badges to pass out for all the teachers from their buildings. I found her with only three folders left. She gave me a distraught look.

"You've heard?" she asked.

"Yes. What can you tell me?"

She glanced around. She motioned me into the nearest room. Maps of the world covered one wall, and copies of old front pages of newspapers from famous days in history were on another. Must have been a social studies room.

Georgette was pale and trembling. "I can't believe this. They can't accuse Meg of this, can they?"

"Did you talk to Meg?"

"Last night—before all this. The poor dear is totally upset. We only talked for about thirty seconds. It was as if she couldn't wait for me to get off the phone. I was just trying to be kind."

"I'm sure she didn't mean to be rude. This is probably the worst thing that's ever happened to her."

"Oh, I understand. She's been through hell. I hope they leave her alone. I want the old Meg back."

I wondered if that would ever be possible.

"What happened to Belutha?"

"I don't know everything, but I know more than most." Georgette obviously loved being the center of mystery and intrigue. "I had to be here early and I talked to Robert Tusher. I do not like that man. When I'm near him, all I can think of are venomous snakes."

"Did he find the body?"

"No, one of those community service kids did. Tusher

had to be here first to open the school. One or two other custodians and a couple of those working delinquents came in at the same time. I don't like having those teenagers around. They're criminals, you know."

I wasn't about to argue with her.

"Each was told to open different rooms. This place is so new, they wanted everybody to be able to tour. I think they had photographers scheduled to be here from the local papers—now there is going to be a mob of them. Mabel, the secretary here, said they had calls from every news organization in Chicago and the suburbs. They are going to be doing some of those remote broadcasts 'live from the scene' in front of the school. There's nothing anyone can do to stop them."

"Which kid found her and where and what happened?"

"Veronica Heskwith, a girl who is supposed to be a senior here, but has only enough credits to be a sophomore. She was sobbing in the office when I walked in."

"Do you know anything about her?"

"She doesn't have a reputation as a troublemaker. I heard she just failed classes here, but did her juvenile delinquent activities outside of school."

"What did she say about finding the body?"

"Nothing at the time. The poor girl just sobbed and sobbed. Mabel told me that the body was in the new library. Belutha had her head bashed in."

"With a book?"

"I don't know."

"Is there anything else you've been able to find out?"

"No. All these wild rumors are out of control. Don't people have any sense?"

"I guess sometimes not."

"This is a tragedy."

"Is school going to be canceled?"

"I don't think so. Carolyn is going to make a speech in a few minutes. She's supposed to explain everything to the staff when she talks." Georgette glanced at the clock. "She's going to be starting in a few minutes in the auditorium. You should be there."

I hurried out. Teachers were scattered in knots around the doors and in the hallway outside the auditorium. I looked inside. The room could seat at least a thousand people. The slightly less than three hundred teachers were joined by every employee in the district, bringing the total crowd close to five hundred, counting custodians, bus drivers, secretaries, clerks, and teacher's aides.

The room buzzed with talk. No one was on the platform, and events didn't seem to be anywhere near starting. I went in search of my liars Beatrix and Trevor.

I found Beatrix talking to Seth.

I said, "Beatrix, I need to speak to you."

She gave me a dirty look. "I'm going into the auditorium."

"You don't have to talk to him," Seth said. "He's not going to be grievance chair or building rep after the election."

"Seth, angel, dear, sweetheart, sit on it and rotate."

His mouth gaped open at me.

"Beatrix, you need to talk to me right now, or I will find the nearest police officer and begin talking to him or her about you."

"What about?"

"Now, Beatrix. We need to chat. In front of a crowd or in private?"

"I can come with you and be a witness," Seth said. "You don't want him sexually harassing you."

"He's gay," Beatrix snapped. "I can handle any man, much less him."

"Beatrix, let's not try my patience this morning."

I looked back at the area around the auditorium doors. People were still milling about.

We stepped into an undecorated classroom.

"What do you want?" she demanded.

"Belutha told me you were meeting with people after the big fight at the PTA meeting. You told me you left. Now if Belutha told the police, they would have questioned you about it. Why did you lie to me and why didn't she tell the police?"

"The police questioned me."

"And what did you tell them about having a meeting?"

She hesitated and her eyes shifted left and right.

"You didn't tell them about that meeting, did you?"

"Belutha is dead. She can't tell anybody anything."

"Which means you had a reason to silence her, but why did Belutha keep silent?"

"Wait! I misspoke. What I mean is . . . Well, so what if I met with him?"

"It's where you were," I said, "and the timing of the meeting that make a difference. I'm sure the police are going to question me. I visited Belutha last night, and she told me, but not the police. I'm sure the police will find that interesting."

"You can't prove what she said. You could be making this all up."

"Now, Beatrix. You need to tell me the truth about what you did Monday night."

"I . . . I . . ." She began to cry. "I . . ." She reached in her purse and pulled out a tissue. "I met with Trevor after he met with Jerome. Then I talked with Jerome."

She glanced up at me. This was news indeed. I'd assumed I'd been talking about only Trevor. She must have presumed Belutha had told me about both meetings. Which meant Belutha had held out on me as well. Being no fool, I hid my surprise.

"What did you say to Jerome?"

"I met with him to pledge him my support. He was delighted and happy. He promised he would get me everything I wanted."

"How is that possible, Beatrix? No matter how much you have gotten in the past, you've always wanted more. If you got this, you wanted that. If you were given something to shut you up, you found something new to complain about."

"You don't have to be mean."

"Did you promise Seth your support as well?"

"I try to talk to everyone."

"You lied to me, Beatrix. Meg's in trouble and I'm going to make sure she's exonerated."

"Where was Meg at the time of Belutha's murder?" she countered.

"I have no idea."

"Well, you better find out. I heard she was around school last night."

"That sounds like a stupid rumor. Who told you that?"

"I don't remember."

I figured she was making it up. "Let's try remembering about Monday. Why didn't you tell the police about your meeting?"

"I didn't have to tell them. They never asked me about it. Belutha did call me last night and asked to meet with me."

"What happened at that meeting?"

"I arrived at her house around eleven. She was gone. I didn't wait for her."

"Kind of late to be calling."

Beatrix burst into sobs. "You've got to help me, like you help Meg. I didn't kill either of them. You've got to help me."

"Why?"

"Why would I kill Jerome? He'd just promised me everything I wanted. He said he'd file the grievance for me about the field trip. Something you wouldn't do."

"Where did you meet with him?"

She hesitated, glanced at the door, and began sobbing in earnest.

"You met him in the library, didn't you?"

"Yes." She pulled out several tissues and blew her nose. "I'm sure I wasn't the last person to see him alive. Other people were supposed to meet with him."

"Who?"

"I know that Trevor was around. I talked with him myself. I did not kill Jerome or Belutha."

"A possible meeting with Belutha and a definite meeting with Jerome, so far unreported. You sound like a suspect to me. I only have your word that he agreed to help you. How do I know that's true?"

"Because I told you."

"Don't get startled here, Beatrix, but why should I or the police believe you?"

"You wouldn't tell them what I told you?"

"I might."

She rounded on me. "But you visited Belutha. You said so earlier. The police will be suspicious of you, as well. You have as much to worry about as me. If you help me, I'll help you."

"I'm not telling any lies for anybody."

"You've got to help me."

"After all the misery you've put me through over the years, why should I help you?"

"You're the union building rep. You've got to help."

"Being union rep does not mean I am your slave, your secretary, or your knight in shining armor."

"You're a beast." She marched to the door and walked out.

In the corridor I saw teachers streaming toward the auditorium, so I headed there myself. I took a seat in the back with some other members of the English department. Up on the podium Carolyn's face was grave. The crowd hushed when she approached the microphone.

She welcomed us briefly. "You are all aware of the two tragedies that have occurred in the district. I am not free to discuss the case, but we are cooperating with the police. Frankly, I don't know much about their investigation. I would ask you not to speak to the public or the press about these events. It is likely that the press will try and trap you into an unfortunate statement. If someone wants to interview you, please direct them to call me. There is no need for you to be bothered by a reporter or to be concerned about your safety. We obviously need more than the current alarm systems and we are going to have a security firm in here. We will also be revising entrance rules and access. I guess we're a more urban school than we cared to admit. For today, we will follow the schedules you received in your folders. Your building administrators or department chairs have the information you need. As of now, school will definitely be in session tomorrow with a crisis team available for students or teachers who want to consult with them."

Carolyn made a variety of other announcements. I looked in my folder at my schedule for the day. The faculty from Grover Cleveland had a meeting, immediately following Carolyn's remarks, with Edwina in this room.

After Carolyn reassured us and said some kind words for the departed, teachers from the other schools left the room. Edwina took the podium. She was given to delivering cheery pep talks on the first day of school. I sat through a half hour of her rambling in which she avoided mentioning the murders but was less perky than usual.

Next we had a departmental meeting back at Grover Cleveland. Jon Pike gave me his most toothy smile when I entered the classroom assigned for the meeting.

He began the meeting by quoting *The Tempest,* act 2, scene 2, lines 40–41: "Misery acquaints a man with strange bedfellows." Which almost made a little bit of sense. Did this mean he didn't like any of us? That the deaths were misery and we were all in this together? Rachel Seebach put her hand over her mouth and laughed silently. Several other people in the department exchanged quizzical looks or rolled their eyes.

Next Jon began passing out the School Improvement Plan. This is another joke perpetrated by the Illinois state legislature. Over the years the teachers of Illinois with their administrators have written Directed Learner Objectives, Behavioral Objectives, Rubrics, and all kinds of other bureaucratic horseshit. It is legitimate for a community to want to know if their children are learning. It is beyond passing strange for the state to insist every few years that we reinvent the wheel. The real problem was that many of the Republicans in the state legislature are basically racist and determined to beat up on the city of Chicago and the teachers' union there. An example of the bureaucratic madness—for some grade levels there are now nearly a month's worth of tests to be given: nationally normed tests, Criterion Reference tests, Illinois Goal Assessment Plan tests, high school placement tests, and on and on—during which the students are not taught.

Jon explained for thirty minutes about the School Improvement Plan and what we were supposed to do about it over the year.

Rachel whispered at one point, "Let's cram all these up his ass."

I laughed. Jon gave me a dirty look.

He ended the meeting with, "Light seeking light doth light of light beguile." I thought this might be from *Love's Labour's Lost.* Since it made no sense and there wasn't going to be a quiz, I ignored it.

Before I could rush away, Jon asked to see me. We met in his classroom. The walls were covered with posters of Shakespeare and playbills from performances of the bard's work. A replica of the Globe theater sat on the windowsill.

"Tom, I wanted to see you. We're going to have to change your schedule."

"What?"

"The electives you teach are two of our most popular subjects. We can't have you teaching them. With the controversy around you, we can't risk having kids quit them."

"Have any left?"

"Two so far in each."

Besides the slow kids, I taught two honors electives: the Modern Novel and Short Story Writing.

"You can't switch them this close to the beginning of the term."

"Sure I can. I'm the head of the department."

"What if some kids took those classes to get me for a teacher? Won't they be disappointed and try to leave?"

"Perhaps." He considered for a few moments.

"Don't we have to discuss assignment changes at a departmental meeting?"

"I don't want to turn this into something political or some kind of power struggle."

"Why don't we see what happens this semester and then discuss any changes near the end of the term. I'm sure you'd want to use proper procedure. People get annoyed when you don't."

"I guess."

All gay people know homophobia can be quietly insidious just like this. It wasn't blatant discrimination. Just hidden, covert, glass-ceiling discrimination. We just didn't get the more prized positions. Gay rights laws will help, but this kind of thing would be impossible to stop. He said he'd wait to make changes.

After our departmental meetings, we were supposed to either do curriculum work based on what Jon had just told us or work in our classrooms. I hoped to be able to do the latter if I got done talking to everyone I needed to.

Plus, eventually the police would learn about my visit to Belutha, if Beatrix wasn't filling their ears about it at that very moment. It could be a conspiracy theorist's field day with Meg and me seen in cahoots to do in dastardly enemies. I tried calling Todd, but he was in a meeting. This wasn't an emergency yet.

I went hunting for studly Trevor. I found him in the cafeteria with a bunch of younger teachers. I know it's because I'm getting older, but some of them did look barely out of their teens.

I walked up to Trevor and draped a more than companionable arm around his shoulders. I said, "Trevor, we need to talk."

He gave those around him a pained look.

"Aren't you Tom Mason?" one of the young women asked.

"I am."

"I saw you on all those shows. What was Oprah like?"

"As kindly as she appears to be."

"Oh. Are you and Trevor friends?"

"That's up to Trevor. He and I need to chat."

"I need to get to a meeting," Trevor said.

"You're having a break. Let's take a minute. I'm sure you'll find the few moments profitable."

He couldn't refuse without looking ugly and ungracious. Those of us into politeness need to be wary. Those who wish to take advantage will use our penchant for politeness against us. As I did now against Trevor.

We found an empty storage closet.

"What was all that crap? Don't ever put your arm around me again."

"You sound awful pushy for someone the police are going to need to talk to."

"What do you mean?"

"Before you trotted off to a bar to meet your friends, you had sessions with Beatrix and Jerome the night he was killed."

"Who told you that? It's not true."

"What were you and Beatrix arguing about the night of the murder?"

"We . . . she told you? Beatrix blabbed?"

"Beatrix is not a person I would pick to confide in."

"I should have picked you? I tried that. Remember? You weren't very responsive."

"Because I didn't want to date you means that I'm not somebody who can be confided in? You have to learn to stop thinking with your prick."

"Why am I still talking to you?"

"Think of all the wonderful advice you're getting and imagine how much better you are going to feel when you get this sordid confession off your soul."

"I have nothing to confess."

"What did you and Beatrix fight about?"

"That bitch didn't tell you?"

"I didn't say it was Beatrix who told me."

"Belutha. She saw us. She told you? This place is crazy, like an Italian court in the fifteenth century. Do I need to have someone taste my food before I eat it?"

"That depends on how important you assume you are, doesn't it? You lied about leaving. I think the police would love to hear about that. Let's make this a nice easy threat. You tell me or I tell the police."

"What makes you so damn confident I won't just walk out of here?"

"You're young but sensible. You're a gay man. Generally, if we make it out of our teen years, we have a remarkable sense of self-preservation. Enlightened self-interest will tell you that talking to me is better than being grilled by the police."

"Maybe I like a man in uniform."

"Good for you. Now it's time to talk."

"If you must know, although it has nothing to do with the murder, I talked to Beatrix about the union. I had to meet with Jerome to protect myself. He promised me that if he was elected, gay people would be protected. Beatrix asked me to support Seth in the election. She told me if I didn't, she would personally tell everyone on the school board that I was gay."

"Surprise for you. Jerome was a stealth candidate for the religious right. He was going to do a great deal to harm a lot of us, especially you and me and whoever else is gay or lesbian in the district."

"He lied to me?"

"Straight through his teeth. He'd have promised you anything to get elected. I think he'd been making promises to just about everybody to get their support. Welcome to the real world."

"I had to promise Beatrix to support Seth."

I could have sworn Beatrix told me she was on Jerome's side. Could Beatrix have exacted promises from both men to insure her support and double-crossed both of them? I felt a slight twinge of admiration for Beatrix's boldness and duplicity. I also wondered how stupid she thought people were. In a still relatively small district, did she think people wouldn't notice? That Jerome and Seth might never talk? Then again, their paths would generally not have crossed, except once a year in a large group like today. Maybe Beatrix saw it as a calculated risk that could pay off. She could always call one of them a liar. Her sympathizers would rally to support the poor put-upon Beatrix.

"When did you talk to Jerome?"

"After the voting started. We had set up the meeting earlier in the day. You gave me no concrete assurances that I wouldn't be fired. I had to have something."

"He gave you concrete assurances?"

"Yes."

"Like what?"

"He promised I'd get tenure."

"And you believed him?"

"Why shouldn't I have?"

"Look, twit for brains. We're gay. On the whim of the district, tenured or not, we can be fired. He didn't have the power to ensure tenure for anybody, and tenure isn't some magic wand for gay people."

"But I thought tenure protected us."

"More bad news. Tenure only means they have to go through due process to get rid of us. It is amazingly easy for someone not to be given tenure or to be tenured and then fired."

"That's not the way it was explained to me. They can't hurt me if I'm a good teacher, can they?"

"Yes, they can. Whoever explained it to you is under the same misconception I was until I became building rep and learned the true state of things."

"Being gay and teaching is nuts. It's too much pressure."

"It sure feels that way sometimes. Jerome was a right-wing zealot who was pulling your chain to get your vote."

"Do you enjoy being an insulting know-it-all? And that was mean to put your arm around me. Everybody could see it."

"I'm thinking of putting my arm around the shoulders of a different man on the staff each day. By the end of the year they can be making up rumors about nearly every guy on the faculty. Then I could start in on the custodians."

"I don't think that's funny."

"Neither is murder. Where did you talk to Jerome?"

He hung his head and whispered, "In the library."

News indeed. I needed to lighten up on my little friend, who'd just boosted his rating on my suspect list.

"He was alive when I left," Trevor asserted.

"Do you know who else he was waiting for?"

"No."

"Did you notice a purse?"

"No. Why?"

"Meg said she went back for hers."

"You mean you're questioning her story?"

"I haven't talked to her directly. What kind of mood was Jerome in when you left him?"

"Calm, nothing special. He just made the promise to me. How could he lie like that straight to my face?"

"I don't know. Some people get so desperate to win an election they will tell any lie that pops into their heads. Did you see anybody in the hall when you left?"

"No. It was quiet."

"Did anybody see you leave?"

"I don't think so."

"What time was it?"

"I didn't look at my watch. I'm sure it was before eleven."

"You've got no alibi for the murder."

"You're not going to try and pin it on me? You're not going to tell the cops? I had no reason to kill him or Belutha."

"Unless they had both threatened to keep you from getting tenure."

"Look, Mason, I'm just a guy trying to keep a job. Why hassle me?"

I didn't get the sense that he was a killer. A liar, a closet case, a mild celebrity groupie, a party boy who wanted to get his rocks off whenever he could, but not a killer. "You'll probably have to tell the police the truth at some point. When they piece together who the real killer is, they'll need to have the whole sequence of events down clear."

"It's going to look bad that I lied?"

"Yep."

He sighed. "This is too much. I wish I was straight. If I was straight, this never would have happened. If I get out of this okay, I'm going to find a closet and stay in it forever."

"That would be unfortunate."

"Yeah, well, you don't have much say in what I do to protect myself."

"If you don't want people to think you're gay, I'd suggest a different tailor."

"Why?"

I pointed at his iridescent gray vinyl pants with black polka dots. "The black silk shirt is suspicious, but you could probably get away with it. However, those pants scream, 'I'm a faggot.' I think they make you look very sexy, but the fashion police might want to interrogate you about them. I do know that if you wear them to school—straight or gay, the kids will think you're a swish from the get-go."

"You're always so morally superior. Judging those of us who are more closeted than you. Don't you ever get tired of it? You think you're such hot shit. Who are you to get so high and mighty? Your lover's been in one of the biggest closets in the country. You may be famous, but you and your lover have some of the same problems I do." He began walking out.

His comment surprised and irritated me. "I'm only trying to help Meg," I began, but he was gone. I reflected on what he'd said as I walked down the hallway. In my haste to protect myself and find the killer, had I stepped over the bounds of decency? I'd have to think about that later.

I found Georgette in the middle of a gaggle of secretaries near the school office.

"Have you talked to Carolyn?" she asked.

"Does she want to see me?"

Georgette motioned me aside. She lowered her voice. "Mavis thinks something odd is going on."

Hard to put one over on old Mavis. A couple murders could bring out the oddness police.

"What do you mean?"

"People have been in and out of her office all day. The police, Lydia Marquez, the president of the school board."

"They're probably just discussing the case."

"Maybe, but Mavis isn't sure. Between every visit, Carolyn is on the phone. She left her office about an hour ago and didn't say where she was going. I think you better find her and talk to her."

"Why?"

Mavis Lukachevsky hurried up to us. "Have you heard? Someone claimed that Meg Swarthmore is in the district."

"Where?" I asked.

"In her library. Working."

"You're sure?"

"It's the latest rumor."

# 12

I hurried to the library. No one was in the open area near the checkout desk. I approached Meg's office but stopped when I heard raised voices. One was Meg's. The other I realized after a moment was Carolyn's.

Meg was saying, "I just came to get some personal things. I did not design this visit as a confrontation."

"You can't be here."

"I'm leaving in a few moments. What has turned you into a raving loony, Carolyn? You were always more sensible than most."

"I've been trying to remember the past," Carolyn said. "I've been trying to piece together why there have been two murders."

"And what have you come up with?"

"Each of the people has some connection to awful things that happened years ago. Some seem like fairly mild tawdry gossip, and I haven't found something back then that could be lethal now."

"And that insight leads you to conclude . . ."

"I don't know." Carolyn paused, then said, "You know Belutha was hit with *Smith's Comprehensive Encyclopedia*?"

The killer had to be somebody who had easy access to the schools and wouldn't be regarded as suspicious.

"Someone got in here again?" Meg asked.

"And took the book and brought it over to the new school," Carolyn said.

"Anybody can get into this school until late. There's some kind of activity here almost every night and on weekends. Even you, Carolyn, have a lot of easy access."

The school's alarm system works only after all extracurricular and community activities are done, which is sometimes not until after midnight. That explained how easy it was to get into Grover Cleveland, but wouldn't there have been a gauntlet to go through to get into the new school? We didn't have security guards or metal detectors before this, and usually such devices aren't put in to protect a building after hours. Mostly they're set up during the day to keep kids from hurting each other.

"The police are checking phone records," Carolyn said. "Belutha started making a lot of phone calls after nine o'clock last night. The police are tracking down who all those were to, and they're going to talk to everybody."

"She didn't call me."

"They think she may have received some calls as well. She has call waiting, so she wouldn't have missed an incoming."

"So what if she received calls?" Meg asked.

"That they were the night she was murdered probably has significance."

"Why'd she make the calls?"

"The police aren't sure. The five-year-old said there was a mysterious visitor yesterday evening."

I wondered if it wasn't about time to hie myself to my lawyer to make sure they didn't accuse me of something, but I wanted to hear all this, and I wanted to see Meg, and I wanted to interrogate Carolyn.

"Why don't we talk about you as a possible suspect?" Meg said.

"I beg your pardon."

"Carolyn, there are no secrets around here. You've been part of this district a long time. You've been in the thick of fights."

"That comes with the job."

"You've lived here for many years. You always act like you're so far above it all, but that hatred around here hasn't missed you. I've thought about you and the past as well."

"What does that mean?"

"Carolyn, you've known Jerome for years. As a teacher, as a low-level administrator, as his principal, and as his superintendent. You were close many years ago."

"We haven't been for years."

"And why is that?"

"People drift apart."

"Something happened many years ago. I've been trying to piece it together. I called my old friend Agnes Davis to ask about it. She vaguely recalls you took several graduate classes with him."

"We used to drive to De Paul together, so what?"

"Maybe you were more discreet than most."

"Save your baseless suspicions for someone who cares."

"Nobody suspects you of murder, Carolyn, because you're the above-it-all superintendent. An old affair gone sour might make an interesting motive for murder."

I'd only heard Meg turn on a friend like this once before, and that was me in the corridor of the courthouse.

Meg was still speaking. "You knew all these people. You weren't in their churches, so that isn't the connection. Were you trying to influence the union election? Trying to get in a candidate who was favorable to you or easy to deal with? Did you get secret calls from Jerome?"

"I talked to both candidates. I always do. I can't believe you're trying to make something out of such nothing."

"What did Jerome promise? Or maybe he struck you as a nitwit and you figured you could manipulate him the easiest. Then when he wasn't amenable to your suggestions, you bashed him."

"What for? I have no motive."

"What happened all those years ago? Were you lovers?"

"Don't be absurd."

"I'm real curious to see the relationship between all the players."

"There is no relationship." For the first time since I'd known her, Carolyn's voice sounded with a tremor . . . of what? Fear? Deep emotion about something.

"No?" Meg said. "I imagine there is. I don't know if the police are going to follow up any of this. With the second murder they might have to. Unless they try to pin it on me."

"Maybe they should." Carolyn sounded spiteful and mean.

"I have no alibi for last night. The cops checked. I was at home. Alone. How about you, Carolyn? Do you have a rock-solid alibi?"

"You shouldn't have come here today, Meg. You're obviously overwrought. I suggest you go home. Let's let a little time pass before we decide on your future."

"Until you came in here today, I thought we were

friends. You won't have to worry about my coming back to work. I've written out my resignation."

I said, "Please don't quit."

I stepped into the room. They both turned to me, and each gave me a distinctly annoyed look.

"We're having a private conversation," Carolyn said.

"I've wanted to talk to both of you about the murder."

"And we've wanted to speak to you." We all turned at this new voice. Baxter Dickinson, the River's Edge detective, stood in the doorway. We all gave him distinctly annoyed looks. This did not make him disappear in a puff of smoke.

He called over his shoulder, "They're in here."

Moments later he was joined by his partner, Leonard Rosewald. He said, "Mr. Mason, if you could follow us, we have a few questions to ask you."

There wasn't any point in fighting about it. I trailed after them to the science office. No one sat out in the corridor waiting to be talked to.

Rosewald began, "Mr. Mason, we understand that you met with Mrs. Muffin last night."

I didn't bother to carry on about "how did they find out" or make nonsensical comments about demanding my rights. I started with everything Lydia Marquez had told me and finished with my visit to Belutha.

"What time did you leave Mrs. Muffin's house?"

"About nine."

"You have any proof of that?"

"My lover can tell you what time I got home."

"I saw you guys on television," Dickinson said. "I've seen Scott Carpenter pitch a few times. I'm not so sure how interested I am now in seeing him play."

"That's because you started betting on baseball games, and he cost you money," Rosewald said. "I told you betting on baseball had the worst probability statistics and predictability of any sport."

"Can we get on with it?" I asked.

"You in a hurry?"

"I want to talk to Meg."

"We've tried talking to her once about this new murder. Your lawyer has her well trained. She said nothing. We'll be talking to her again with her lawyer present if necessary. Right now we're concerned about you."

"I need to go." I got up and walked toward the door. "You'd arrest me except you've traced her movements after I left her."

Dickinson nodded. "But you may need to go with us to the station," he said. "Do you want to talk there or here?"

"Look, try those *NYPD Blue* tricks on someone else."

On that show, they would seldom solve a case if the people they brought in for questioning simply exercised their right to demand a lawyer. With their mixture of bullying and wheedling, the cops on the show convinced many a poor sap to give himself up. I knew I didn't have to stay.

"We need to go over your statement," Dickinson said.

"With my lawyer present from this point on. Good-bye." They did not shoot me in the back for trying to escape.

I'd wasted half an hour with them. No one was in the library. I walked over to the district office. Mavis told me Carolyn had put out the word that she wanted to talk to me.

I sat in her office. She barely glanced in my direction. She drummed her fingers on her desk. "How long were you listening to Meg and me?"

"Long enough to hear you both accuse each other of having possible motives for murder based on something that happened in the past. After listening to you and Meg, I'm not sure who or what to believe. As an administrator, you've been decent, but as a friend, Meg's been wonderful."

"She didn't look like she wanted to talk to you."

"No, she didn't," I admitted.

"We could do this as a trade. I give you information, you give me information."

Lydia and me, Belutha and me, Carolyn and me—all sharing—I could have my own personal support group.

I said, "We can try it."

"Why did the police want to talk to you?"

"I was the mystery person who was at Belutha's house."

"Why did you go there?"

"Lydia Marquez gave me a tip about the fights among the three friends. I wanted to follow it up."

"Who fought?"

While I wasn't sure who I trusted at the moment, I wanted information, and if I had to give some to get it, fine. The police knew everything I was going to say already.

I gave her the information I'd gleaned about Lydia, Belutha, and Jerome.

"I'm surprised," Carolyn said. "I never knew any of this."

"Really?" The doubt in my voice approached the sarcastic.

"Tom, we've gotten along well, but I don't think you should try and take advantage of that."

"You said it yourself when you saw your name on the chart. You'd go after everybody. That's what I'm doing.

Why were you and Meg fighting? I thought you were friends."

"Does a superintendent every really have friends?"

"Yeah, I think a superintendent can have friends. There's no need to hunker down in an office and pretend the world is out to get you. Did you really talk to Jerome and Seth about the election?"

"You must have eavesdropped on nearly the whole conversation."

"Yes. Remember, we were going to trade information? It's your turn." Was she going to go back on her word? "You said you had information for me."

"I did talk to both Jerome and Seth. If I can see a way of easing relations between the district and the union, I'm interested." She gave me a grim smile. "Here's a tip for you. Either one of those two would have been bad for the union. They both quite cheerfully promised to give away the store."

"Why to you?"

"I'm not really sure. I think they were planning to use me in their campaigns."

"What on earth for? An endorsement from the superintendent can't have much effect in a union election."

"Yes, but they didn't seem to know that. It seemed very important for them to curry favor with me, although that Seth is totally blind to anything but his transfer policy. He wanted to make all the teachers in the district rotate assignments."

"Is he nuts?"

"I think he'd give up tenure for all the teachers and half the salary raises of the past twenty years, just to get his way."

"What's the background with you and them?"

"Seth I don't know. While I was working on my doctorate, Jerome was taking some administrative classes. We drove to school together for a couple semesters. We became friends of sorts. We talked about religion sometimes. I even attended his church once or twice, but I couldn't get into their intensity or fervor. He seemed disappointed, but not heartbroken. That was it. We drifted apart after that."

"That hardly seems a terrible secret that needs to be withheld at the price of politeness and friendship."

"Proving the absence of an affair is nearly impossible. Meg was snarling at me from the moment I entered her office."

"Why?"

"I asked her. She told me to leave her alone."

"That is so not like her."

"Yes."

"Were you supposed to talk to Jerome the night of the PTA meeting?"

"I was going to meet with both of them."

"Did you?"

"As you know, things got out of hand. I had no time."

Carolyn could help no more. I left.

I hunted for Meg but didn't find her. When I asked Georgette if she had seen her, Georgette looked hurt. "She turned her back on me and walked away."

"I'm sure she's still too upset to talk," I said. "When things calm down, she'll be thinking more clearly." After spending a few more minutes reassuring Georgette, I wandered to my classroom.

I entered warily. I stood at the door and checked as best I could the placement of everything. Nothing seemed out of order. So far so good. I stepped farther into the room. I saw a note taped to the top of the computer monitor. I opened it with the tips of my fingers touching it only at the edges. It was from Rita Fleming. She had fixed my computer. I turned it on. It hummed pleasantly to itself. I tried several CDs and the hard drive. Everything seemed perfectly normal.

I tried sitting at my desk. No tacks on the chair. I leaned my elbows on the desk. It crashed to the floor. If this was a comedy sketch, this would be the funny part. I wasn't laughing. Papers covered the floor past the first row of student desks. My coffee cup had spilled its cold contents on a stack of computer disks. While I fumed, I began cleaning the mess.

Moments later the door burst open. It was Kurt.

"Somebody said there was a terrible noise down here." He pointed to the desk. "What is that?"

I held up one of the legs. It had been sawed off and replaced under the desk, as had the other three.

Kurt chuckled.

I still wasn't up to the humor of the situation. Kurt, seeing my displeasure, tried to stifle his mirth. He helped me pick up the papers that had scattered when the desk fell. I checked the drawers. They were empty. I no longer had tape, grading pencils, thumbtacks, paper clips, masking tape, overhead markers, and a hundred other little items.

"I've been cleaned out."

He came and looked over my shoulder. Together, we did a careful examination of the room. Hidden in the bottom of a storage cabinet was a pile of all the materials from the desk.

"It's a joke," Kurt said.

"Why would somebody be doing this? It's past the

point of silly harassment. Mixing it in with death and destruction is poor timing at best."

"Have you found out anything that would clear Meg?"

I sat at my desk and began replacing all the items in their proper spots. I wasn't going to waste my time trying to get the police to take fingerprints off them. Finding usable prints would be unlikely. They had murder to deal with. Who cared about practical jokes? I did, and I was tired of it. I wasn't sure what the point was of replacing this junk in a broken desk. Perhaps it was reassuring to have stuff in its normal place.

I answered Kurt's questions about the investigation. After I finished, he said, "Your buddy Beatrix cornered me again."

"Can't we just take her out and shoot her?"

"She keeps things interesting."

"Beatrix seems to have outdone any person in history for duplicity." I told him about her getting concessions from both candidates.

"Amazing. I didn't imagine Beatrix had it in her. I knew she was stupid, but boldly stupid. I am impressed."

"Carolyn was trying to work the candidates and they her. Jerome and Seth were truly desperate." I filled him in on that part of the conversation.

When I finished, he said, "I had more hopes for Carolyn. That seems faintly unethical."

"I thought it was a little out of the ordinary. Then there's the Trevor Thompson mess. The poor guy is scared out of his mind about losing his job. He either needs to find a bigger closet or switch professions. He'd promise either Jerome or Seth his support for guarantees about his job."

"There are no such guarantees."

"We know that. He didn't. What is going to happen with the election?"

"I talked to the local office. They left it up to us. For a while I was thinking of making it a hereditary monarchy, but I heard some kindergarten teachers are planning a coup d'état and are going to declare a dictatorship."

"I can hear tanks rumbling in the streets."

"I wouldn't mess with a bunch of kindergarten teachers. Anybody who can deal with five- or six-year-olds on a daily basis is tougher than anybody I know on this planet. So who killed Jerome and Belutha?"

"Somebody connected these people back in the past. Everybody, except for Trevor, fits in. I have lots of information, but it is not complete. If it came from Lydia Marquez, I've assumed all along it was distorted. Now I don't know if I should have believed any of it."

"Would anyone know the total connection?"

"I'm not sure. Normally, I'd try Meg, but I haven't been able to talk to her. What can you tell me about this Beorn Quigley?"

"He was one of the assistant coaches on the football team for a few years. While I was athletic director, I recommended to the administration that he be dropped."

"Why?"

"He began trying to run everything as if it were a marine boot camp. Calisthenics were turned into an endurance contest. I think the boys were afraid of him. Fear as a motivation on the athletic field has lost some of its cachet in the last few years."

"What kind of teacher is he?"

"He's got a couple shop classes. I've never heard of any complaints from him or about him from anybody. He got bent out of shape at the administration when he lost the coaching job. He calmed down some when I told him I was the one who recommended he be let go."

"What did he do when you told him that?"

"Mostly he looked kind of confused and lost. At one point he did vow to run against me in the next union election. He never did. Too lazy? He got over it? He's just an all-around mope? I don't know."

"The administration ever say anything to you about him?"

"No. I know he worked in the district as a custodian during the summer for a few years. His family has that feed-store business, but he didn't work there that I know of until you told me."

"He was a custodian. He could have had keys or certainly access to them."

"Possible."

"I want to talk to him again."


I found Quigley in the shop area. He was sharpening saws. He gazed at me. If it weren't for his face, he'd be put in a calendar for leather and butch men. He had a mature/muscular/sexy look. However, I would have voted against the tattoos on his forearms.

He nodded a greeting and picked up another saw and began to hone the edge.

"I'd like to ask you a few questions."

"Okay."

He continued sharpening. I waited for the loud grating noise to halt for a moment, then asked, "Could you stop that a minute?"

He put the saw down next to him on a bench. The shop

area was basically a large garage. One entire section was for car repairs. Each semester they got a used-car business in the community to donate a wreck that the classes would spend the semester taking apart and putting back together. The shop teachers got to use any profit from the sale of the cars to buy more tools for the department. Furnaces for the school took up another quarter of the room. Immediately around Beorn and me were wooden tables with vises, saws, hammers, and other tools scattered about. On the walls were hooks and nails with the outlines of tools to show which piece of equipment went where.

Beorn's gray steel-rimmed glasses glinted in the fluorescent lights. I noticed his hands were extraordinarily large. Plenty big enough to grasp a large encyclopedia. His hands had streaks of oil on them, and they glinted with tiny shards of metal from the saw sharpening. Next to him was a pair of gloves.

I said, "I heard you were a custodian in the district for several summers."

"That why you came down here to talk to me, to discuss jobs? I doubt it. Just say whatever it is you've got to say and be done with it."

"The murders had to be done by somebody with access to the schools. As a custodian you'd have had a chance to handle keys. You could have made duplicates or kept a set, or you could have found ways to circumvent the security system."

"Not in the new building."

"Aren't you scheduled to be teaching over there?"

"All the shop teachers in the district rotate. I take a few classes that don't fit into other schedules. I got one here and two there. Depends on your specialty. They don't give us keys or instruction manuals for disarming the alarm system because we're going to have classes over there. You think I killed those two?"

"Did you?"

"No."

"Where were you last night?"

"With a friend."

"All night?"

"From eight in the evening on."

"Do you have keys to this building?"

"No."

"I was told your family didn't get along with the Marquezes and the Muffins."

"That was my parents."

"But it must have affected you."

"Why must it have affected me?"

"Because then you would know details that would fill in some of the things I was missing about the background of all the people involved."

He almost smiled. "My mother and father died in their early sixties. Of natural causes. My father had a stroke. They were very involved in the community. My dad ran for mayor years ago and lost the election. I think Lydia Marquez was part of the reason he lost."

When I moved to town, I wasn't all that interested in the local politics of River's Edge. I spent most of my time running to Chicago working with various gay organizations on equal rights bills in the Chicago city council and the Illinois state legislature.

"How was she part of it?"

"It was more than working in a campaign. She was younger then, but her tactics were the same. Nowadays, mostly, I happen to agree with her politics. Back then Lydia was from a faction we didn't want to take control. My father and his friends had been in charge for a long time. River's Edge was like their perfect little small-town America. It didn't make any difference that housing subdivisions were beginning to hem the town in on every side. This was utopia. Lydia was part of the faction who were outsiders who didn't want to keep it like it had been when we were growing up. Look what's happened since they gained control. Growth is out of hand. No planning seems to go into anything. Houses are built too densely together. The streets can no longer handle the traffic. Have you tried to get into Orland Park anytime on a Saturday?"

"You murdered them because traffic is bad?"

"I guess you must enjoy making sarcastic comments, but do you really think they help you get anywhere? You play all these put-down games, but nobody likes it."

"Who's nobody?"

"I don't."

He picked up a saw and began testing the edge.

"And is picking up that saw supposed to be some kind of threat? Am I supposed to be impressed with how tough you are and stop asking questions because you can rub your thumb over a sharpened blade?"

"No, actually, I'd just picked it up at random. It wasn't meant as a threat." But he didn't put it down. "What did you expect me to do? Saw you to death?"

"I'd put that crack in the sarcasm end of the spectrum."

"I'm taking lessons from you."

"What happened with the election with your dad?"

"People were angry. People's feelings were hurt. My father never forgave them for the lies they told."

"Lies?"

"That's how they won the election. They made up stuff about my dad. It was like a national election. Rumors went around that he was unfaithful to my mother. My dad was no saint, but he never cheated on my mother. There were rumors started that he was secretly meeting with developers and was going to sell out the community. Of course, when their side won, they couldn't get to the developers soon enough to start plowing under everything this community had ever been."

"You must be really angry at Lydia and Belutha and Jerome."

"Yes."

"But how could you come to the meeting and make those statements that make you sound like a Nazi?"

"I'm very conservative. I can have those beliefs. I agree with Ms. Marquez, unfortunately. I didn't vote for her in the election, but I voted for the other three candidates. They represented changes I think should be made in this district."

Trevor Thompson walked in. He and Beorn exchanged a look. I glanced at Beorn's ring finger. No little band of gold.

"I'll be through in a minute," Beorn said.

"What's going on here?" I asked.

"Don't talk to him," Trevor said.

Secrets and closets, oh my. "You two know each other?"

Beorn answered, "Trevor and I hang out together sometimes."

"You're gay?" I asked Beorn.

He shrugged.

"Don't talk to him," Trevor said.

"Will you cut that out," I said. "I want to find out what the hell is going on here."

"Get used to disappointment," Beorn said. "I don't parade my private life in front of anyone. I don't think you should be parading your sexuality in front of everyone. If you kept it quiet, I wouldn't mind."

While Beorn put away all the saws, Trevor stood next to the door. I got no more information about past history from Beorn.

# 13

I decided it was time for a Meg confrontation. She'd been downright nasty. She had answers I needed to have.

I called Scott. I told him I'd be home after talking to Meg. He wished me good luck. Outdoors, the break from the summer humidity continued. The refreshing breeze was from the north. The humidity had been dropping all day. If you didn't have a classroom that faced south or west, you might be able to get through the day tomorrow.

My truck was fine. I drove to Meg's. She'd lived in Frankfort for a short while, but moved back to River's Edge a few years ago.

I saw her car in the driveway. She answered the door. She was dressed in a purple sweat suit and sneakers. I got a look that would have withered the soul of the worst student discipline problem.

"I'd like to talk, Meg. It's important. You know it is too."

She moved away from the door. She left it open but did not invite me in. I followed her.

We stood in the middle of her living room.

I began, "I don't understand what it is I have done so wrong that has made you so angry."

"You silly twit. Haven't you figured it out? I did bash Jerome with that book."

"Oh." I sat down. "You killed him?"

"Yep."

"Then why did you hide that second book in my room?"

"I didn't. The police mentioned it, but it made no sense to me. I refused to answer their questions, so they refused to give me any explanations. I like your lawyer and his advice. What book?"

"There was another copy of *Smith's Comprehensive Encyclopedia* in the back of one of my cabinets with blood and everything. It had no fingerprints on it except for mine. I inadvertently touched it when I found it."

She sat down. "How odd."

"What happened that night?"

She gazed out the front window at the flowers and shrubs she'd planted around her house. I let the silence go beyond the uncomfortable. She didn't seem to notice.

"I didn't plan to kill him. It just happened. He wanted to make me convince you to support him for union president. He threatened me."

"With what?"

"In the first district I worked in the teachers called a strike. I crossed the picket line. That may not be a tragedy, but I've always been ashamed of it."

"Would you really bend to that kind of threat?"

"I did indeed refuse to bend to that kind of threat. He got vicious and mean—called me a scab. I've always felt ghastly about my behavior then. It's why I quit that district and why I've been so pro-union since. I was trying to make up for it. At any rate, he and I were both out of control. Much worse than in the meeting. Finally, he picked up a book and threw it at me."

"Then it was self-defense."

"No, I ducked and laughed at him. He screamed at me at the top of his lungs and told me I'd be sorry. He'd made me so angry that when he turned his back, I picked up the first book that came to hand. I took a running start and smashed him one from behind."

"How could that be the first book? The body was halfway around to the other side of the room."

"That was so odd, and now you tell me about this other book." She shook her head.

"Belutha was bashed with another volume of the same encyclopedia."

She smiled briefly. "How ironic."

"I heard a rumor you were at school last night."

"Checking everything?" Her smile was cool. "I was home. Alone."

I cleared my throat. "I don't get something. How did he get to that odd corner of the room? You said you ran after him. Did you chase him?"

"No. He walked past the checkout desk. I hit him there."

"There was no blood near the checkout desk."

"I know."

"Meg, what's going on?"

"I'm not sure why I'm telling you. Maybe I'm just tired of holding in the truth. I couldn't tell the police I hit him— that stupid I'm not. After I bashed him, I tried to revive him but without success. I remember kneeling next to him listening to the quiet. I remember hearing the clock over the checkout desk tick and thinking about my mother's funeral. Sort of odd, but I wasn't thinking clearly at that instant. Then I ran to the nearest washroom to get some water to try and revive him. He was breathing when I left. When I got to the washroom, I didn't have a cup with me to carry any water. I had to run to the teachers' lounge to get something to hold water. I couldn't have been gone more than five minutes. By the time I got back the body had moved.

"I figured maybe he'd awakened on his own and had simply got up and left to find the police to press an assault charge. I was sure he would.

"That's when I noticed the books on the floor. I walked around the room and there was his body. The book I'd hit him with was next to him. He was dead. I noticed a few dark smears that I realized must be blood. I hadn't seen any when I hit him. I thought I might have just missed the blood the first time. There wasn't all that much. I thought it was odd, but I figured maybe he recovered long enough to stagger around the room, probably fallen again, and hit his head on something. Even if that was true, I'd still be implicated for the initial hit."

"Had you really forgotten your purse?"

"Actually, yes. I also had a meeting set up with him. No one was supposed to know about it. That was Jerome: if you have a choice, always tell a secret.

"I thought it was kind of odd, but I presumed I killed him. That's why I didn't want you investigating. I was afraid you'd figure it out. Now, I just out and out told you. I can't imagine why you'd want to still be a friend or why you'd want to investigate the murder."

"Maybe you didn't kill him."

She gazed at me for a brief moment, then smiled. "That's kind of you to be loyal. I guess I shouldn't have snapped at you at the courthouse, but really, what choice did I have? You were going to stick your nose in it and make it worse. If by some miracle I didn't kill him, I realized that I was capable of harming another human being. I always thought of myself as a rational, thoughtful person if not an outright pacifist. How could I be driven to such an extreme?"

"He must have made you very angry."

"He kept denying reality. That drives me bonkers. Trust me. When people are willfully stupid, I get loony."

"Willful stupidity as a felony offense. Works for me."

I actually got a small smile out of her.

"Listen, Meg. It's not easy to think of yourself in a different light. Violence can be frightening. It may not be easy to accept, but you need to give yourself time. We're all capable of it, even if we don't want to face it. You also need to think right now. Certainly, you hit him and knocked him out. You don't remember blood from that first time. Maybe there wasn't any. Maybe someone came in and finished the job."

"I can never prove that."

"I've found out that there are a lot of secrets that all these people have been harboring."

"Dead is dead. Down is down."

"Belutha said she saw you in the hall. I hadn't heard you left before the end of the meeting."

"Where was I going and for what?"

"Well, yeah."

"Just trying to cool off and do some deep breathing. I know that doesn't sound dramatic, but it's true."

"How did your purse get next to the body?"

"I was in such shock, I thought I must have put it there."

"But it was lost. How could you have?"

"I guess I just must have."

"I've got another question. How did the book get next to him?"

"What?"

"When you hit him, where did you put the book?"

"I'm not sure." She thought a minute. "I was in such shock, I don't remember. I must have just put it down on the counter."

"When you came back with the water, you didn't pick up the book?"

"No."

"Try this instead, Meg. You bash Jerome. You run off. You were gone, what, five minutes?"

"At most."

"Meanwhile, the killer comes in. Moves the body."

"Why?"

"I don't know yet. The body is moved for whatever reason. The killer must have been watching and listening from behind the stacks or in the hall. Using gloves or only touching the edges of the book, he or she bashes him again. This time blood is drawn. The murderer takes your purse and puts it next to the body to add weight to the prints you have left on the book."

"Why put that book in your room?"

"That book in my room is more proof you didn't do it. The killer wanted to add me as a suspect. You wouldn't implicate someone else in something you did. It had to be pure accident that the killer happened upon your quarrel."

"Serendipitous murder? I guess it's possible. I didn't think I'd kill somebody. Why do you think I wouldn't try and implicate someone else?"

"Did you?"

"No."

"If you wanted to implicate me, you'd have put both

books in my room or wiped one off completely and left only the one in my room. The killer wanted to implicate both of us. So, the killer takes another book and wipes off the prints and bashes him again. He or she had to be planning on the spur of the moment. Under those circumstances, it's easy to screw up."

"Why wipe off the prints?"

"So that I would be implicated as well. The killer couldn't put my prints on it. Whoever it was had to simply eradicate all of them."

"That's an awful lot to do in a short period of time."

"A person drags or carries the body to the back. The killer took the book with your prints on it to finish the job."

"And gets another book? And does it again? And risks capture?"

"Maybe it was an afterthought."

"And why drag the body to the back?"

"To avoid being discovered? If the killer heard someone come in while he or she was dragging the body, it would be easy enough to plausibly say they were trying to revive him. Jerome gets bonked a second time. Was the part where you told the cops you called 911 true?"

"I called after I found him the second time."

"Did you examine the rest of the library?"

"No."

"Maybe the killer was in there while you examined him." She shuddered.

"Or maybe he or she was there all along. Or maybe you simply left too soon. The killer didn't have time. It is possible you really misplaced the purse and the killer found it or was bringing it back and finding Jerome out cold changed everything forever. Adding the purse would point to your guilt."

"That sure worked. How did the killer know I wouldn't just stay there or even begin to search the library? I could have stayed put or found a custodian right outside the door. The killer would have been trapped."

"Maybe the killer was ready to bash you as well. Not a lot of time to plan and think, if it was a crime of passion."

"Mine was."

"While you were with the body, you were in danger. Whoever it was waited for you to leave both times. Maybe the second time was when the killer decided to try and implicate me as well. If the murderer was improvising, then he or she could have been making all kinds of mistakes. We don't know yet that the cops aren't going to try and pin part of this on me."

"Why would you murder Jerome?"

"General principles? He was too stupid to live?"

She actually smiled. "I hadn't thought there was a possibility that I wasn't the killer. Thank you for giving an old friend some hopes. It's most kind, but it is useless."

"Why?"

"Even if I didn't kill him, I'm going to prosecuted for assault."

"By whom? Your victim is dead. He's not going to care. All we have to do is find the real killer."

"I don't have that kind of energy. The theories you're expounding are just a little too unbelievable. If you try them on the police, they'll laugh you out of the station. Maybe even try and include you in as an accomplice. I wouldn't bother, Tom. I know what I did.

"When Todd drove me home, he didn't ask all kinds of silly questions, which I couldn't have answered then anyway. I think I'm going to call him and tell him I'm prepared to plead guilty. It would be too humiliating to go through a trial. I'll take my punishment. If I received the death penalty, I'd probably die of old age before they got around to executing me."

"I think it's a little premature to pick out the correct execution attire. Even then, the murder wasn't premeditated. You'll be around for quite a while. There is more to this than either one of us knows so far. I'm going to get to the bottom of it. You should call Todd and tell him all this."

"I will."

"I'm going to keep investigating. What I'm trying to find out is what is this big secret or secrets that people are dancing around."

"There is another secret I have."

I wasn't eager to hear more confessions. I could barely handle what I'd heard so far, but I prepared myself to listen.

"I was part of the problem with the Quigleys."

"Beorn told me that his dad died of natural causes."

"I was young and foolish, perhaps half his age. He was prominent in the community, the head of the school board. He got me my first job here. We had an affair. I thought we were so discreet. We had our tryst in Chicago, when the Conrad Hilton was still the Conrad Hilton, not whatever it is today. It was bliss, but it ended after our first real date. What happened was an election. His opposition threatened to tell about us. They wanted him to withdraw. It would have meant divorce and disgrace. He was a pillar of the community when the scandal broke and he couldn't take it. The first I knew about it was in the papers. I was married at the time."

Old Meg had a secret affair as a young adult. Hidden fires indeed. That Beorn remembered it differently, I didn't doubt.

"In fact that was what led to the divorce. Before it became public knowledge, somehow my husband found out. I'm sure I was much less clever than I thought I was. I would have left town, but I certainly wasn't going to go crawling back home to southern Illinois. My husband left me, and I only had my paltry income from working in the library."

"But why does any of this have an effect now?"

"Lydia and Belutha and Jerome somehow found out. The three of them wanted me to turn on you. They wanted me to tell secrets about you. I'm not sure I know any to reveal. Do you dress up in women's clothes?"

"Not even on Halloween."

"Well, that's the kind of information they wanted. I was to help them against you. I refused. By trashing you, they hoped to be able to trash Kurt and all that he'd done with the union."

"Why? He wasn't running again."

"But Lydia, Belutha, and Jerome wanted to run against his record. You can't imagine how desperate they were. Or maybe you can. You've met them and you know that type of person. Even a race for dogcatcher can bring out the worst in people. They were using it for revenge—to get even."

"I feel like I'm living in Morons R Us. Were there no lengths to which any of these people would not go?"

"And if they wouldn't, their friends would egg them on. One person after another would tell the latest rumor, each more fantastic than the other. It would make them more desperate to win. As their anger increased, their rhetoric heated up, and they did more and more outrageous things."

"Why didn't Seth and Jerome ever just talk to each other?"

"It's either high stupidity or religious fanaticism, which

is basically the same thing, I guess. I think they actually wanted to get together, but winning the presidency was also part of Lydia's and Belutha's faction attempting to control one more elective office. Jerome couldn't back down. His buddies had made a commitment."

"What tangled webs we weave. Sorry, Jon Pike is getting to me." I told her what he'd threatened to do.

"It never ends, does it?" Meg said.

"Nope."

"One last thing. I feel bad I couldn't tell Agnes the whole story that night. I hope I didn't get her into any trouble."

"She's fine. Worried about you like we all are." I stood up. I gave Meg a hug and said, "I'm going to try and get a good night's sleep tonight so I can be fresh for harassing suspects. Call Todd and tell him everything. He'll know exactly what to do. Meanwhile, don't give up hope."

She smiled wanly and thanked me.

I drove home as the north wind was rising to a gale. I had the window down and my arm draped over the edge. It was deliciously cool. I pressed the remote control switch on my key ring to open the outer gate. I pulled into the driveway and shut off the headlights. I stopped to listen to the silence and watch the twilight deepen to night. The early stars began to glow. The rim of an orange moon began to peak over the horizon. I let the car idle forward into the garage. I entered the house through the breezeway into the kitchen.

All the electric lights were off. Two votive candles were burning on the table. The smell of garlic and rosemary filled the air. The windows in the living room were partly open admitting the refreshing air. A fire of applewood and sage burned in the fireplace.

215

"Honey, I'm home" didn't seem like the right thing to bellow out.

I loosened my tie and draped my sport coat over a chair.

I found Scott in the library. All the walls had built-in bookcases to the ceiling. The only gaps were for the windows and the door. A set of leather-covered furniture clustered in the center of a Persian rug.

He was reclining in a brown leather chair. A reading light was on next to him, and a book was open on his lap. He was gazing out the window at the rising moon. The heels of his black leather boots rested on each end of an ottoman. He was wearing black leather pants. You have to have the right build to wear leather pants, and if you're sitting down in them, the slightest bulge of a love handle will show. Scott looked perfect. He wore no shirt but had a metal chain around his neck and a leather band around his right biceps. A visor of a leather cap hung low over his forehead. Another fire was in the fireplace. I could smell the leather of his pants and the chairs.

Definitely not a "Hi, honey, I'm home" outfit.

I could see my reflection in the windows and I presumed he could too. He spoke to my reflection. "Hi, Tommy."

I sat down on the floor between his legs. I felt him move them as pillars on each side of me. He leaned down from behind and finished untying my tie and placed it with his book on the teak end table. He was rereading *The Wind in the Willows*.

He placed his hands on my shoulders and gently kneaded the muscles. He murmured, "I was reading the part where Mole stops Rat so they can go to the hole Mole abandoned. His old home."

I leaned my head back into his crotch and listened to the gentle flow of his words as he described the scene almost verbatim. I lost myself in the rhythm of his thrumming baritone. I began caressing him. After we finished, we had a dried-out but not burned dinner.

Scott had made a trip to the city. He had had a conference with his banker, broker, and accountant and then stopped at his penthouse. I filled him in on the latest developments in the case.

"I like thinking she didn't do it," he said, "and I sort of respect her for being willing to bash him a good one."

After the dishes were done, we both put on gym shorts and white socks. He wore a Bullwinkle T-shirt. I chose one with a University of Oz logo—tiny ruby slippers, and a small witch flying against the background of poppies and the Emerald City. We sat in front of the fireplace in the living room.

We were discussing the murder. "I think the body being moved convinced me," I said. "Somebody doesn't just stagger around then plop over dead."

"I don't know," Scott said. "That seems kind of possible to me. The first blow might have made the subsequent ones more effective."

"The book being moved tells me she's innocent."

"If Meg was telling the truth."

Reluctantly, I agreed.

Scott said, "Meg's at least partly guilty."

"We're all capable of violence and we all have those feelings. What about when you aim at a batter's head?"

"I've never beaned anybody intentionally."

"But you've hit a few guys?"

"Yes."

"Meg just went a little farther. Since it wasn't in the context of a game, she couldn't possibly get away with it."

As we lay in bed later reading, he the article "Sport Contracts" his lawyer had given him, I, *Entries from a Hot Pink Notebook,* I said, "You know, I'm a little worried about the kids' reaction tomorrow. The 'high school mind' is not usually set to be receptive to openly gay teachers."

"I bet the reactions will startle you or rather the lack of them. The vast majority simply won't care."

"The insecure idiots will feel compelled to make a statement. They always do."

"Yeah, you can't predict which way they'll jump. High school kids are emotionally volatile."

"Got that right."

# 14

First thing the next morning, I checked my room for further sabotage and to do any last-minute preparations for the imminent teenage onslaught. The humidity was back and the wind had died. The breeze made feeble attempts to puff through the opened windows. Everything seemed fine until I tried to turn the computer on. Nothing worked. I began punching keys and softly swearing. The door to my room opened. It was forty-five minutes before school was to start, and I didn't expect anyone. A slender kid about five feet eight inches in dark horn-rim glasses stood in the doorway. He carried a computer disk in his shirt pocket—the pocket protector of the nineties.

"Can I help you?" I asked.

He looked behind him in the corridor, then eased several steps into the room and shut the door. He looked solemn. "Mr. Mason, if it's okay, I wanted to say thanks for all you've done."

"For what?"

"Being on television and everything. I feel better about myself because of you. I think you and your lover are really brave. The gay kids I know are really proud of you."

"Thanks," I mumbled.

He glanced nervously around. "I can't stay long. I also came to give you some information." He edged a little farther into the room.

"What's your name?"

"Jason Brewer. I don't have a lot of time. I heard that a few of the kids are going to be out to get you."

"What do you mean?"

"Like, when you walk down the hall, to more than accidentally bump into you, or slash the tires on your truck, wreck things, stuff like that."

"Who told you this?"

"Lots of kids know. I heard it from three different sources. Friends of mine. They wouldn't hurt you, but everybody knows what's being said. The only thing I could tell for sure was that it was some of the troublemakers here at school."

I banged my hand on the top of the computer. "I don't need the hassle."

"You could hurt the computer if you do that."

"Doing what?"

"Banging on it."

"The stupid thing isn't working anyway."

"It's not plugged in."

I glanced at the floor and the wall. I felt silly. The cord and outlet were near him. He took several steps forward and reached down.

"Jason, wait."

But it was too late. He plugged the machine in. Several things happened simultaneously. The computer screen lit up for a second, then the insides fizzled, and puffs of smoke rose from the back. Jason was hurled against the wall. He slumped to the floor.

220

As I rushed to his side, smoke alarms started to sound. He was no longer in contact with the electricity. He was breathing. Moments later several custodians with fire extinguishers rushed in. The computer fizzled a bit and let out a last puff of smoke as they thoroughly doused it and the surrounding area.

It took the paramedics seven minutes to arrive. Jason hadn't regained consciousness by the time they took him away.

Edwina arrived to assess the situation. "You are kind of a menace," she said.

"Wrong again, O wise leader. The people who did this are the menace. The victim of the crime is not the guilty one."

"Yeah, well, we can't have this going on all the time."

"Which means, I'm sure, that you're going to dedicate yourself to finding who is responsible."

"If I could get rid of you, it would be a lot easier."

"Edwina, did you involve yourself in the school board elections?"

"I didn't care enough to be involved. I've got two years and three days until I can take early retirement."

The bell rang and the distant murmur of voices and slamming lockers began moments later.

"You can't teach in here today. The police will have to examine everything."

I held up the unplugged chord. "Somebody frayed the connection."

She didn't even glance at it. She said, "With the new school in operation we have enough empty space here that we can find someplace you can use temporarily."

"Did you think about getting one of those community service kids to keep watch like I asked you?"

"Little late for that now."

"Better than nothing. I can't stand guard."

She gave a martyr's sigh. "I'll see what I can do."

"When?"

"I'll do it." She left.

I wound up in an old art room. The only student behavior I noted as even mildly threatening or different during the morning was almost a nonincident. It happened as the kids were streaming out of fourth-hour class to go to lunch. One student, notable only for his short, baby-fat-covered body, was about to be the last one to exit the room. In a stage whisper he said, "I don't want to be the last one out. I don't want to be in the room alone with him."

And they were gone. A demeaning insult, but what would be the point of making an issue of it? And why is it always the fattest, ugliest, and most unattractive straight, white males who think people are interested in them sexually?

I stopped in the office to call the hospital and find out how Jason was. He was out of danger, but they were keeping him under observation. If he was still in the hospital later, I would try to visit him. I called Scott and told him about what had happened. He promised to keep checking on Jason.

Edwina told me Frank Murphy was waiting to talk to me in my classroom.

Frank got right to the point. "It's a good thing you were there so early. It narrows down who we have to question."

"Couldn't somebody have come in overnight?"

"We're working on people who had access. Fortunately, it's a short list."

"Could it have killed anyone?"

"Very possibly. That kid was really lucky."

A uniformed cop walked in with a male teenager whose shoulders slumped, acne festered, and head hung.

"Which one is this?" Frank asked.

"David Blake, one of the community service kids. The only one who was working as a custodian this morning."

"An adult could have done it," the kid said with a snarl as irritating as a buzz saw.

Frank said, "You were supposed to be polishing floors in the newer wing. Two adults say they saw you come down this corridor this morning."

"Who? Nobody saw me. I . . ."

"Just goofed," Frank finished for him.

"That don't mean nothing."

"The kid who plugged in the computer might die," Frank said.

"I didn't kill nobody."

"We don't know that yet. If you can tell us who's behind all this, maybe we can go easy on you."

"Wasn't nobody behind nothin'. It was just a couple of us messing around. Nobody was gonna get hurt. Wouldn't have if Mason had kept quiet about who he is. It's his fault for opening his big mouth."

Silence equals safety mixed with the "it's the queer's fault" defense. I was torn between wanting to punch him and pitying him for how pathetic he was.

Frank's good at eliciting information from reluctant teens. Before the end of lunch the kid was in tears and had given Frank two more names of the saboteurs—one of whom was a computer expert.

Near the end I asked, "Which one of you put the bloody encyclopedia behind the books?"

The kid gave me a blank look and asked, "What encyclopedia?"

No kid is that good of an actor. If I was any judge after all these years of teaching, his uncomprehending look was genuine.

The next hour was my planning period. First I stopped in the library and counted the *Smith's Comprehensive Encyclopedia*s. There were now three of them. I wandered down to the office to talk to Georgette.

She smiled at me. "I talked to Meg a few minutes ago. She told me how you'd been so kind. What can I do to help?"

"It looks like they caught the saboteurs from my room, so that's one less headache. As for the murder, I'm convinced it has something to do with the relationship between all these people years ago."

"Back when?"

"When all this union business started. It seems to have gotten mixed with all the anger in the community."

"I can tell you about the union. I was here then." She looked around. "I can get Adele to answer the phones. It's time for my lunch anyway."

We sat in the little room off the office that the secretaries eat lunch in. Georgette took hers after everyone else so we were alone.

"What exactly happened so long ago?"

"I was an assistant secretary in one of the elementary schools back then. We were all petrified about what to do if the union called a strike. We'd been warned that if we didn't cross the picket line, we would all be fired."

"There was going to be a strike at the time the union was formed?"

"Yes, it was a mess. The teachers had demanded the right to have a collective bargaining election. The school

224

board kept putting it off, in hopes of staving off the need to negotiate that year, but the teachers went to court and forced them to have the election. There was a big fight between three factions, the IEA, IFT, and no union at all. Agnes was leading the IFT faction. She seemed to have the most support at the high school. Beatrix was leading the IEA faction and was more popular at some of the elementary schools. After Beatrix won the election, everything around here became chaotic. She can organize a classroom like nobody's business, but she just cannot handle people. She knows how to complain, but not how to run things. The teachers turned down the settlement that the negotiations team came back with. I remember it was something like a one percent raise. When they went back to the negotiations table, the board laughed at them. The teachers then voted to strike. That lasted half a day. Beatrix had no idea what to do. She wouldn't listen to the advice she was getting from the IEA. The board was ready for the strike. They had mobs of parents in all the buildings and substitute teachers in half the classrooms. Some teachers crossed the picket line. I called in sick. I know that's a coward's way out, but I couldn't betray my friends. The strike failed. The teachers wound up getting no raise at all. Everyone was furious. The parents who'd gotten involved on the board's side tried to get some of the teachers fired. The teachers threw out the IEA and got the IFT in. The high school teachers have been in control of the union ever since. Most of the teachers are gone from back then, but people can carry grudges a long time."

"I never knew most of this." I also wondered a bit about Agnes Davis's explanation about what had happened all those years ago. She'd left out a lot of information. I wondered if it had been deliberate.

"You started about ten years after it happened. The old guard was tired of fighting by then. Things were quiet for so long. People quit or retired."

"Was Jerome involved in that election?"

"I don't remember specifically, but everyone was involved somehow."

"Who was in charge of the no-union camp?"

"Carolyn Blackburn."

I raised an eyebrow.

"She kept trying to make peace between all the factions. She would meet with one side, then the other. Several sides accused her of selling out. I heard rumors that the school board wasn't all that united either, although I've never been able to confirm that. Carolyn did everything she could to make things work. Nobody was willing to listen. The next year she started working on her administrative certificate."

I thanked Georgette for all the information and returned to class. My room was now free. An odd moment happened when I was unlocking my classroom door. The halls were extremely crowded with the changing of classes. I realized I'd left a plastic container from my lunch in the faculty cafeteria. Instead of proceeding directly into the room, I turned to go back. Out of the corner of my eye, I saw an elbow swipe past where I would have been. In the swirl and eddy of students, I couldn't tell who had done it. Perhaps it was nothing.

After school I went in search of Beatrix and found her in her classroom. She gave me a hostile look. Her "What do you want?" came with as good of a snarl as the most accomplished teenager.

"I'm not here to accuse you. I was wondering if you would tell me about the big union fight back when you were all getting the organization started here in the district."

"Why should I?"

"Because I think it has something to do with the murders."

"How could it?"

"I don't know. I do know that you've been busily threatening everyone or making duplicitous promises around the district. I know you promised both Seth and Jerome your support, and you've been badgering Trevor. Is there nothing you would stop at to get your way or cause trouble?"

"That kind of crack is supposed to make me want to confide in you?"

"I'd like to hear your side of the story."

Meg walked into the room accompanied by Edwina.

"What are you doing here?" Beatrix snapped at Meg.

"Last night Tom and I talked about events in the past," Meg said. "It made me do some thinking."

Beatrix stood up. "What is going on? How can she be in the building?"

"She's with me," Edwina said.

Beatrix said, "I want my union rep here."

"I am your union rep," I said.

She gave me a nasty look. "If my union rep won't protect me, maybe he shouldn't be union rep anymore."

"I'm not here to accuse you," Meg said. "I just want information. Who were the administrators back when you were setting up the union?"

"You should know. Old man Quigley was the head of the board of education."

"Beorn's dad," I added.

They ignored me.

"But wasn't there a religious faction at that time too?"

Meg asked. "Not like the vocal and obnoxious one we have now. Back then I recall they were simply in favor of the status quo. But who was it on the board who was in favor of the teachers? I've never been able to figure that out."

"Why is it important?" Beatrix asked.

"I'm not sure."

"I haven't the faintest notion."

Meg said, "But you've been making deals left and right during this union election. You were union president back then. You should have known who your friends were. As I recall, you aren't shy about meeting with people. Who did you try to double-cross then?"

Beatrix spoke to Edwina, "Why are you letting her speak to me like this?"

"It kind of amuses me," Edwina said.

"What happened in that election that you lost?" Meg asked.

When Beatrix spoke, her voice changed to an icy rasp. I hardly recognized it. "You want to know what happened back then? I'll tell you what happened back then. I was the one who fought to get the teachers' representation. I was the one who took a stand. I was the one who stuck her neck out. I was the one who led the fight for teachers' rights in this district. What did I get for all my hard work? I got shit on. Agnes Davis, Jerome Blenkinsop, the whole crowd betrayed me. They went around this district and told every lie they could about me. I didn't mind people running against me as union president. They have that right, but they had no right to lie about me to every teacher in this district. I will never forgive them past the day they die. I will hate them forever." Her eyes glittered with tears, but she did not shed them.

"Hated them enough to kill?" I asked.

"Don't be stupid. Of course not. I have nothing more to say. I'm leaving."

And she did.

The three of us looked at each other, then at the door Beatrix had slammed.

"Was she angry enough to kill?" I asked.

"I don't want to be involved," Edwina said.

"Thought I had something there," Meg said.

"I'll keep checking it out," I said.

Meg turned to Edwina. "As my keeper, you may lead me out the door."

"Uh?" I said.

"I was told I can't be in the building without an escort."

"Are you okay?"

"I talked to Todd. For a taciturn, distant, formal man, I find him very reassuring." I watched them walk down the corridor. I returned to my classroom. Everything I'd planned to do today now had to be set up for Monday. I wanted to give out books, syllabi, pretests. I also wanted to go over first-day-of-school writing assignments. I don't use "my summer vacation" as a topic, but I do like to have a sample of their writing so that I am aware of their skill level. For my classes of slower students this is especially important so I can design individual programs. It doesn't hurt for the bright kids either. Their essays aren't up to the level of Montaigne yet, and I can get some idea of what items to cover to make them better writers. Ever since some idiotic bureaucrat in the state of Illinois enshrined the five-paragraph essay as the norm for proving the ability to write, I've had to work twice as hard to teach the bright kids the elements of real writing. To any dopey bureaucrat reading this—I've never written a five-paragraph essay about anything. In the real world neither has anyone else.

I'd long since given up bringing papers home to grade. Which meant spending extra time at school on a Friday going over them. Today, I made sure at least one other faculty member knew where I was, and I notified the custodians of my intention to stay late. The new security officers hadn't been hired yet, but I wanted to make sure my presence was recorded by as many people as possible.

Half an hour into the essays and I was ready to go nuts. Not from their length or general content, which wasn't actually all that bad. It's the little things that teenagers have been doing wrong for years that cause me to see double. I'd just noted the fourteenth use of *alot* as one word. We aren't talking "pet peeve" here, we're talking "driving me bonkers."

Just after four o'clock my classroom door opened. Lydia Marquez walked in. She was dressed in a conservative business suit. She seemed almost hesitant as she walked about halfway toward the desk.

"May I disturb you?" she asked. Not a hint of demeaning nastiness. I nodded at her. "I heard what happened in here today. I'm terribly sorry. No one should have to be worried about that kind of attack on their job."

"Thanks," I said.

"You told Belutha and the police everything I told you. She called me that night and the police talked to me today."

"Did you expect me to keep silent?"

"No, I guess not." She sighed deeply. "You know, you and I aren't so different. We both believe very strongly. We both refuse to compromise our essential principles."

Was she here to make peace? I said, "I wish it wasn't necessary to fight."

"With me?"

"I wasn't actually thinking of that, but that too. No, I meant, I get tired, as must you, of always having to rush to the barricades to defend against an attack from another direction."

She leaned against a desk. "You got that part right. Don't get me wrong, I do want to win every battle in the worst way, but there does always seem to be a new one each time you get to the horizon. Just once, I'd like to reach a new dawn and realize there were no more fights to be fought."

"Absolutely."

"Do you stay this late all the time?"

"Not usually. Because the day was hectic, I needed to go over a few things to be ready for Monday."

"You're a dedicated teacher."

"I'm not unusual. Most of the staff in the district is very hardworking."

"I guess you're right."

"I'm curious," I said. "Why is it so important to you to try and lead the charge to get Meg fired?"

"But I'm not leading that. I've had nothing to do with it. As far as I know, that's coming from Carolyn Blackburn."

Carolyn must have been more hurt by Meg's words than I thought.

I said, "What do you know about the elections way back, when they were setting up the union?"

"That was before my time. I only heard about them secondhand. I'm not even sure I remember much of that. Our church was a little dinky thing back then. The old pastor used to tell tales from years ago. At the time they only had ten adult members of the congregation. Now we have nearly a thousand."

"What did the old pastor used to say?"

"Oh, dear, well, I'm not sure. He's been dead for five years. Did you know he was on the school board at the time they voted in the union?"

"Really?"

She nodded. "He was a good and kindly man. He always tried to get people to work together. On the school board he told us he tried to produce a compromise among all the factions. That was before we realized the power of the family and the word of God."

"Somebody said Carolyn Blackburn was working extremely hard at that time to get the sides to reach a compromise."

"I believe I heard that she was. She's been helpful so many times. Why in the recent election—" Lydia stopped abruptly.

I stood up. "In the recent election what?"

"Nothing." She began to fidget.

"Carolyn was on your side?"

"I didn't say that."

"She was trying to influence the election? Are school superintendents supposed to do that?"

"I can't believe you would be so naive not to think anyone in a district who is going to be affected by an outcome wouldn't be doing all he or she could to affect that outcome. Carolyn was always working to make this a better place."

"And save her job by making an alliance with your faction?"

"And what would be wrong with that if that's what she was doing?"

"It's an easy way to get herself fired by the faction she didn't support."

"I think I've said enough." Lydia began edging toward the door.

I called the elementary school and asked if Seth was still in. If anybody would be around on an opening day, it would be an elementary teacher. High school teachers are mostly likely to be gone the instant the kids leave. Grade school teachers tend to hang around and work. He was in.

I drove to his school. He frowned at me when he saw me.

"I wanted to ask you something," I said.

"Don't bother, I'm dropping out of the election. They're going to have to get somebody else to run."

"Why?"

"It's too dirty. I've got people trying to get me to lie or listen to their lies."

"I heard Beatrix promised you and Jerome her support."

"That's what finally decided me to quit. It's too much."

"You weren't above telling a fib or two. Did you talk to Carolyn Blackburn about the election?"

"What's wrong with that?"

"You don't see an ethical dilemma in speaking to the superintendent about a union election in which she is not supposed to play a part?"

"She came to me."

"She said you came to her and offered to sell out the union."

"I did not. What was I supposed to do when she came

to talk to me, tell her to go away? Besides, she agreed with some of my positions."

"Speaking of, you really wanted every teacher in the district to rotate assignments? Are you nuts?"

"It would be fair."

"You are nuts."

"I don't have to listen to your insults." He walked out of his classroom and turned left. I turned right and walked to my truck.

# 15

I wanted to stop in my classroom. While unlocking the door, I caught a glimpse of something out of place down the hall. I thought we'd put an end to problems in and around my classroom. I hurried forward. In a recess in the wall at the turn to the next hall, I found a male teenager languidly propping up a row of lockers. I'd seen his elbow and foot sticking into the hallway.

"Taking a break?" I asked.

"Nah. Mrs. Jenkins, the principal, told me I had to sit here and watch for people. Nobody told me different, so I've been here since after school. It's boring."

"Did you see anybody?"

"Not much after all the kids left. A few custodians were around. Some woman went into one of the rooms. I think it might have been yours."

"Do you know who it was?"

"No."

"Can you describe her?"

He tossed his hair out of his eyes and rubbed at the acne on his chin. "A big woman. I've seen her around once or twice."

Lydia?

"Young or old?"

"Older, kind of silvery hair. Maybe she works in the district office. I don't know."

Carolyn? I thanked him and went to check my room. Everything seemed to be in place.

I walked to the administrative offices. Wisps of humidity crawled over and around me. The school had been bearable today.

Mavis smiled at me and said Carolyn was on the phone. I told her I would wait. Fifteen minutes later I was shown into Carolyn's office.

"Are you all right?" she asked.

"I'm okay. I'll stop at the hospital on my way home."

"I heard they're going to keep Jason overnight, but only as a precaution. He should be fine."

I sat in a leather chair on the opposite side of her desk. "I just had an odd talk with Lydia Marquez," I began. "She said you were the one trying to get Meg fired."

"Not true. Lydia's either making it up or the rumor mill has gone into overdrive."

I guess I believed her. "I also wanted to ask you about the election when they set up the union. I think what went on then had something to do with the murders."

"What on earth put that idea into your head?"

"As I've talked to people, they keep mentioning enmities that go back a long time. There seems to be a lot of focus on that. It was ten years before my time, and I've never gotten the whole story."

"Well, there were actually four rounds of voting." She explained, "The first was to vote to have a union. The second was on the contract, the third to go on strike, and the fourth to throw Beatrix out and put in Agnes Davis as president."

"Those must have been bitter times."

"They were. Nothing anybody could do would lower the rhetoric on either side."

"Several people have said you tried to work out a compromise."

She leaned back in her maroon, leather, high-back, swivel chair. "They are very kind to remember. I always try to get people to work together."

"But you were the head of one faction. The one that wanted to have no union. How did that work? You must have been disappointed."

"After I lost, I was fed up enough to go into administration. This was not a pleasant place to work at that time. A lot of people quit in the years immediately after the election. Things would be far more bitter here if all those people had stayed on. I figured I could have more real influence on education if I got into the administrative end."

"Including in the recent school board election?"

"I beg your pardon?"

"I understand you were trying to influence the outcome. I think I know how you could be on Lydia's side. The board is so out of control now, you're less than a figurehead. You must be terrifically frustrated. Did you figure if they got in, they'd have to lean on you to learn what to do as a school board? You could get your rightful place back. Of course, if the current school board found out about that now, you could be in some hot water."

"Everyone has a right to support who they want in an election."

"And everyone in a public position takes the consequences of their public acts. Or were Belutha and Lydia trying to work that knowledge of your involvement to their own ends? Were they threatening you?"

"Don't be absurd."

"It's not absurd. Everybody's been running around with secrets. Seth says you came to him. You say he came to you. Were you trying to involve yourself in the union election too?"

"What good would the endorsement of the superintendent do in a union election?"

"I don't know. Maybe you've been harboring resentments ever since your faction lost all those years ago."

"Why would I care about back then?"

"I know people in their nineties who can recall wrongs they've felt as children as if they had happened yesterday."

"I've done my best to cooperate with the union."

"You said Jerome and Seth wanted to wreck the union. Maybe you were willing to help in the tearing down."

"The union was no friend to the teachers in this district. We'd all have been better off if there had been no union."

"Who did you tell that to? Who wanted your support that badly? Who would be nuts enough to believe it would make a difference? Who would buy into that madness? Jerome?"

She rose to her feet. She pointed at the door. "Get out." Her voice was soft but icy cold.

I remained seated.

When she realized I wasn't moving, she said, "I can still get you fired."

"What were you doing in my room this afternoon?"

She sat down abruptly.

"One of the kids saw you. Edwina must have ordered him to keep watch. After the kids were caught, she never told him not to. What were you doing there?"

"I can go into any room in the school."

"Let's not be absurd. What purpose would you have to go into my room?"

"Perhaps I was simply looking for you."

"It's far easier just to call down on the intercom," I said.

"No, I'm not the problem here. It looks more like you've got the problem. Who would have access to all the schools and who was around at all the correct times for the murders? You've been involved with all these people, then and now. You've got secrets you're holding back, but I bet if we got all those people together, we'd get a picture of a superintendent losing her grip."

Carolyn swiveled her chair so she could look out on her portion of the potholed parking lot. Below the window was a low shelf jammed with papers and a variety of boxes. She spoke without turning around. "Education these days is not worth the effort it takes to make it work right. Something always goes wrong. There's always another parent who isn't connecting with reality, or a lunatic board member, or a pissed-off teacher to contend with. It's as if there is a world full of Beatrix Xurys. There really doesn't seem to be much point in trying to do a good job. Take you for example. You're no prize. There's always something about you. An issue, a problem. I was a better teacher than you ever were."

Rambling aimlessly wasn't Carolyn's style.

"I've seen more difficulties and dealt with more problems than you can imagine. I've had issues that you could never handle. I've had to be tough and strong. You'd never be able to stick it out long enough. You've got to be able to handle pressure in this job. I was the one who wanted to get Meg fired. I couldn't have her around. That much hassle is too much. I made a mistake."

"You left traces of blood—"

She interrupted. "No, you silly twit. My mistake was taking all of this seriously. It's the same problem you have. You believe all this stuff makes a difference. It doesn't, you know. No matter how much you fight, make sarcastic comments, try to be kind to people, convince them, force them—everything eventually goes to hell."

"Is that what happened with Jerome?"

She completely ignored my question. She continued, "The problem is believing so strongly that you have to act before your frustration level hits a point of no return. I was supposed to meet with Jerome that night. I'd found Meg's purse under a coatrack next to the gym. I was planning to return it. When I walked into the library, I heard them arguing and stopped to listen. The things he said were so irrational. My own anger finally got the best of me. When Meg ran out of the room after she hit him, I hurried to Jerome's side. I barely remember what I did. I know I grabbed one of the books, and I know hitting him felt good. I realized I'd used a different book than Meg. I put the other book in your room. I knew I had to do something with it. Behind your books was the first place I thought of. You and Meg are friends. I hoped they'd suspect you both."

"Why'd you move the body?"

"I was afraid I'd be seen from the hallway. I didn't think Meg would be back. My mind seemed incredibly clear, but I was acting, not thinking. I was there when she came back. I don't know what stopped me from killing her.

"Belutha saw me coming out of the library that night. She bided her time, probably planning the best use she could put the information to. The night she was killed, I was already supposed to meet with her. I was afraid of what she knew. I called her from a pay phone. I didn't want the police to ever be able to trace a call between my home or the school here. Belutha wanted to use her knowledge to get me to bend to her will. That was her leverage. That's why she didn't tell the police about who she saw. She was going to blackmail me and anybody else she could. She believed so strongly and she was going to make her wish come true by making us do as she wanted, just like Jerome. People have an amazing habit of doing what they want, not what you want. You can try a million things, but when they don't work out, the frustration is too much. I don't believe any hassle is worth much anymore."

She turned around. She held a gun in an unsteady hand.

I jumped to my feet. "Are you nuts? If you kill me, everyone will know it was you. Mavis and the rest of the office staff know I'm in here."

"That's not my problem." She raised the gun to her head. "Fairness is for shit."

The instant it took to realize what she was doing and then to shout and leap across the desk to try to stop her was too long. The gun made a horrific boom.

The secretaries, the paramedics, the cops, the detectives, the school board members, the administrators—all flooded into the district office. Early on, I latched onto Frank Murphy and sat with him in the empty school board meeting room. He and Baxter Dickinson and Leonard Rosewald spoke with me for about an hour.

Frank's main comment was, "I don't get this stuff about support in the election. What kind of help is one loon on your side?"

I said, "I'm not sure. I think people believe they are building their coalition one person at a time. It takes a while but it can be very effective. Eventually you can switch from incremental gains to an avalanche. At least that's what they hope."

Dickinson said, "What use is a frenzied fight over the presidency of this union? Who on earth would care?"

Frank said, "Obviously these people did."

Until Todd showed up, Frank remained with me and we talked, mostly about kids we'd known in the past, which ones were in jail, who was on probation, who was dealing drugs, who had turned his life around. Based on the information I gave, the cops talked to all the possible people Carolyn might have been involved with. The inferences I'd drawn turned out to be the plausible ones. (Much later a careful inspection of her vehicle would yield traces of Jerome's blood. No gloves were ever found. She must have had the sense to throw them out after handling the encyclopedia. The traces were microscopic, but that DNA stuff is true.) I stayed in the office for around three hours mostly getting depressed. I tried calling home, but Scott wasn't in.

I called Meg and told her the news. She barely seemed relieved. She told me she was just frightened. She wasn't going to fight about her job, she told me, she was just going to resign and take her pension. All the fight seemed to be taken out of her. I said as many encouraging things as I could and promised to stop by tomorrow. I wanted to get home and talk to Scott, but I decided to make a quick trip to the hospital.

I walked into Jason Brewer's hospital room. Scott was standing near his bed. Another teenager was sitting on the bed next to Jason. He quickly withdrew his hand from Jason's as I walked in.

I approached them.

"You okay?" I asked Jason.

"Yeah, they're just keeping me here for observation overnight. Something about my electrolytes aren't in order." He pointed to the other teenager. A skinny kid with nasty acne. "This is Stanley. He's a junior like me. We're . . . friends."

Stanley gave a nervous laugh.

"I heard you solved the murder," Jason said. "It was on the radio earlier that Ms. Blackburn did it. Did she really?"

I nodded and gave them a brief outline. I wanted to get home.

When I finished, Scott said, "Are you okay?"

"This has been a little busier Friday than I'd thought it would be."

We got ready to leave.

"Thanks for coming," Jason said.

Stanley nodded, and his voice gave a teenage squeak as he said, "Thanks for being who you are. You really help." He cleared his throat. "I mean, sometimes it's hard on kids like us. You make a big difference."

As we turned to walk out the door, I saw Jason reaching his hand out for Stanley's.

In the hallway Scott said, "I'd go through all this again. That's what makes the difference. That gay kids know they're okay." I smiled and hugged him. "I would never change anything," he said. "I love you and having you next to me to go through life with." Scott whispered in my ear, "Let's get married."